DIPANGKAR MALLA BARUAH
LAKSHMAN KANUGA

FROM WELLS TO WONDERS

KB KANUGA'S JOURNEY TO BUILD DULIAJAN

BLUEROSE PUBLISHERS
India | U.K.

Copyright © Dipangkar Malla Baruah, Lakshman Kanuga 2025

All rights reserved by author. No part of this publication may be reproduced, stored in a retrieval system or transmitted in any form or by any means, electronic, mechanical, photocopying, recording or otherwise, without the prior permission of the author. Although every precaution has been taken to verify the accuracy of the information contained herein, the publisher assume no responsibility for any errors or omissions. No liability is assumed for damages that may result from the use of information contained within.

BlueRose Publishers takes no responsibility for any damages, losses, or liabilities that may arise from the use or misuse of the information, products, or services provided in this publication.

For permissions requests or inquiries regarding this publication,
please contact:

BLUEROSE PUBLISHERS
www.BlueRoseONE.com
info@bluerosepublishers.com
+91 8882 898 898
+4407342408967

ISBN: 978-93-6783-979-9

Cover design: Daksh
Typesetting: Tanya Raj Upadhyay

First Edition: February 2025

Disclaimer

This book is a work of historical fiction inspired by real events, people, and places. While it is based on the life and contributions of K.B. Kanuga, certain characters, dialogues, and incidents have been dramatized for narrative purposes.

Any resemblance to actual persons, living or deceased, beyond historical figures, is purely coincidental. The interpretations and representations in this book are the author's own and do not intend to harm, defame, or misrepresent any individual, institution, or organization.

The views expressed in this book are solely those of the authors and do not reflect the official stance of any organization, including Oil India Limited. Readers are encouraged to view this work as a tribute to a visionary leader rather than a strictly factual account.

Foreword

What better way to honour the legacy of K.B. Kanuga, the visionary architect of Duliajan, than by documenting his remarkable life journey for future generations to rediscover and cherish? Through this book, the man who transformed a dream into a thriving township comes alive in black and white, allowing us to reimagine his extraordinary contributions to Oil India and beyond.

This tribute, though long overdue, arrives at the perfect moment to inspire and enlighten. It is a monumental effort, and my heartfelt appreciation goes to the authors, Shri Dipangkar Malla Baruah and Shri Lakshman Kanuga, for taking up this noble task. Their work not only preserves history but also pays a fitting salute to a man whose vision and leadership continue to guide us.

To K.B. Kanuga, we offer our deepest respect and gratitude, and to the authors, a big salute for immortalizing his story.

Shri Trailukya Borgohain,

Director (Operations), Oil India Ltd.

Prologue

Part - 1

The story of Kewalram Boolchand Kanuga is not just the story of a man—it is the story of a visionary who helped lay the foundation for a thriving township in the heart of Assam, amidst the burgeoning oil industry. Kanuga, the first General Manager and Resident Director of Oil India Limited (OIL), was a leader whose name still resonates in the streets and hearts of Duliajan. Under his stewardship, the township transformed from a nascent settlement into a model of industrial and residential harmony. The industrial zone, residential quarters, OIL Hospital, OIL Higher Secondary School, Duliajan Club, Zaloni Club, and countless other landmarks stand as testaments to his foresight and determination.

In one of my visits to Delhi, I had the privilege of meeting Shri Lakshman Kanuga, the youngest son of Kewalram Boolchand Kanuga. Our conversation spanned hours, and I was captivated as he narrated the life story of his illustrious father. Through him, I discovered not just the professional achievements of K.B. Kanuga but also the personal anecdotes, struggles, and triumphs that shaped the man behind the legend. Lakshman Kanuga's vivid recollections brought to life the era when his father, against the odds, charted the course for OIL and the township of Duliajan.

I was also fortunate to receive valuable insights from Shri Manoj Kumar Dutta, a respected teacher and writer from Duliajan, whose knowledge about the early days of the township added depth to this narrative. Their inputs, combined with my research, helped me weave together the tale of a man whose contributions extended beyond pipelines and oil wells.

The decision to write this biographical novel was not made lightly. Kewalram Boolchand Kanuga's legacy is too profound to be left to the fading memories of those who knew him. This book is my humble attempt to immortalize his work, to ensure that the generations to come understand the indelible mark he left on Duliajan and on India's oil industry. Through these pages, I hope to take readers back to a time when the oil industry in Assam was in its infancy—a time of challenges, aspirations, and achievements.

Admittedly, I began this journey with only fragments of information—bits and pieces of stories told to me by those who knew him or had studied his work. Stitching these into a coherent narrative required imagination and dedication. I am profoundly grateful that Shri Lakshman Kanuga not only shared his stories but also graciously reviewed the manuscript and approved it for publication. His approval means the world to me, as does his willingness to co-author this novel, lending authenticity to every chapter.

This book is not just a biography—it is a tribute to a pioneer, a builder, and a man whose vision created a community that thrives to this day. It is also a salute to the era of India's industrial awakening, a glimpse into the environment, challenges, and triumphs of that transformative time.

To the people of Duliajan, this is a story of their roots. To the scholars of history, it is an account of the foundations of one of India's great industrial endeavors. To the readers, I hope this tale of perseverance, leadership, and humanity will inspire and enlighten in equal measure.

As you turn these pages, may you feel the spirit of Kewalram Boolchand Kanuga, whose legacy lives on in every corner of Duliajan and in the hearts of those whose lives he touched.

Dipangkar Malla Baruah
Duliajan, Assam, India
Ph No: +91 9435039820, E-mail: dm.baruah@gmail.com

Prologue

Part - 2

When Shri Manoj Kumar Dutta, a writer from Duliajan first reached out to me, introducing me to Mr. Dipangkar Malla Baruah, I could not have imagined the journey we were about to embark upon. That initial phone call sparked a collaboration that would culminate in this heartfelt tribute to my late father, Kewalram Boolchand Kanuga—a man whose life and work continue to inspire.

From our very first interaction, I was overwhelmed by Dipangkar's genuine enthusiasm and passion for this project. His meticulous research, drawn from archives and historical records, was nothing short of inspirational. As we began exchanging long WhatsApp messages, I found myself delving into my own memories, recalling the moments and milestones that defined my parents' extraordinary journey.

It was a privilege to share these recollections—some rooted in vivid detail, others tinged with the warmth of anecdotes passed down over the years. Together, they paint a picture of my parents' trials and triumphs, their unyielding support for each other, and the joys and sorrows that shaped their lives. My father's unwavering dedication to his work and his vision for a thriving community in Duliajan, and my mother's strength and resilience, became central to this narrative.

Their story is not just one of professional accomplishments but also of personal sacrifices and an enduring bond that spanned more than five decades. Through these exchanges with Dipangkar, I felt a renewed sense of gratitude for their legacy and a deep connection to the life they built together.

Being part of this project has been both humbling and fulfilling. It is my hope that this book will not only celebrate my father's remarkable contributions but also serve as an inspiration to those who read it, offering a glimpse into a time when visionaries like Kewalram Boolchand Kanuga laid the foundation for the future.

I feel blessed to have played a part in bringing this story to life.
Sri Lakshman Kanuga
Gurgaon, Haryana
Ph No: +91 9867363974, E-mail: lakshmankanuga@gmail.com

Table of Contents

Chapter 1: Early Years (1912-1929) 1
Chapter 2: The College Years (1930-1935) 8
Chapter 3: Into the Oil Fields (1935-1947) 15
Chapter 4: Digboi Days (1948–1957) 23
Chapter 5: Building Duliajan (1958-1969) 43
Chapter 6: The Roots of Duliajan 49
Chapter 7: Initial Years of building Duliajan - Through Ups and Downs 53
Chapter 8: Heart of Duliajan 68
Chapter 9: The Prime Minister's Visit 71
Chapter 10: The Journey of Progress 78
Chapter 11: The Spirit of Community 85
Chapter 12: The Legacy of Education 99
Chapter 13: A Community's Growth 103
Chapter 14: The Battle for Life 112
Chapter 15: Echoes of Legacy 120
Chapter 16: The Early Retirement 124
Chapter 17: The Kanuga Legacy Continues 138
Chapter 18: Life After Retirement 142
Chapter 19: The Final Farewell 153

Chapter 1:
Early Years (1912-1929)

The relentless summer sun beat down on Sehwan, a small town cradled by the meandering Indus River in Sindh Pradesh.

It was July 14, 1912, and the Kanuga household was unusually quiet, awaiting the arrival of a new life. The silence was suddenly pierced by the sharp cry of a newborn inside their modest brick home. Asudi Kanuga, drenched in sweat and exhaustion, managed a weak smile. Her husband, Boolchand, stood beside her, nervously wringing his hands.

"It's a boy," the midwife announced, her voice filled with relief.

"A boy?" Boolchand's face lit up with joy, the solemn mask he often wore vanishing in an instant. After two daughters, their prayers had been answered.

"Yes," Asudi whispered, her voice barely audible, yet filled with deep affection. "Kewalram... we'll name him Kewalram."

Boolchand knelt beside her, placing a gentle hand on her shoulder. "He's going to do great things, Asudi. I just know it." His gaze shifted to the tiny baby wrapped snugly in cloth, his heart swelling with a father's hope and pride.

As if sensing the significance of his father's words, the baby's cries softened. Outside, life in Sehwan carried on as usual, unaware that a child destined to change the course of India's oil history had just been born.

The Kanuga family lived simply. Boolchand, a clerk, earned just enough to keep food on the table, while Asudi managed their household with precision, stretching every rupee to meet their needs.

Their daughters, Rukmani and Gomi, were much older and doted on their baby brother like second mothers.

"Kewal, come here!" Rukmani called one afternoon as the boy, now four years old, chased a stray dog down the dusty streets, his small feet kicking up clouds of dirt.

He turned with a mischievous grin. "Why should I? I'm not done playing!"

Gomi, standing beside her sister, laughed. "If you don't come back now, Amma will be angry. She has sweets for you."

"Sweets?" Kewalram's eyes lit up. "Alright, I'm coming!" He darted toward them, his legs flying as fast as his excitement.

As they walked back home, Rukmani looked down at her little brother. "Amma says you're special, you know."

"Special? How?" he asked, his innocent curiosity piqued.

"She says you'll do big things when you grow up. You'll make us all proud," Gomi added with a tender smile.

Kewalram frowned. "But I don't want to grow up! I just want to play."

The sisters exchanged a knowing glance and smiled. "One day, you'll understand," Rukmani said softly.

Years passed, and Kewalram blossomed into a bright and inquisitive boy. His love for numbers and problem-solving set him apart from other children. At school, he excelled in mathematics, often leaving his teachers in awe at how quickly he grasped complex concepts.

Surrounded by the love of his elder sisters and the wisdom of his father, Kewalram's path was slowly being paved. Boolchand, a respected figure in the community, often emphasized the importance of hard work and education.

"Kewal, remember," his father would say, "knowledge and discipline are the keys to a good life."

Yet, Kewalram's heart was not always in his studies. His mind wandered to the skies and streets, where he found his true joy in kite flying. On windy afternoons, he would race outside with his kite in hand, determined to be the last one flying as others' kites fell.

"Look, Rukmani!" he would shout, his face beaming with pride. "My kite is still up higher than all the others!"

Rukmani would smile and cheer him on, while Gomi, ever playful, teased him, "You think that's high? Wait until I make a kite that flies even higher!"

When the winds died down, Kewalram could be found playing Gilli-danda, a street game similar to today's gully cricket, his quick reflexes and sharp aim making him a natural at the game. His friends marveled at how far he could send the gilli flying.

"How do you always hit it so far?" they asked, clapping in admiration.

"It's all in the wrist," Kewalram would say with a grin, demonstrating the precise flick of his hand.

These simple childhood games were more than mere entertainment for Kewalram. They honed his competitive spirit, he developed from kite flying, the focus and precision from Gilli-danda, and his sense of teamwork—skills that would serve him well in the years to come.

The bond between the siblings only grew stronger with time. Under the watchful eyes of his sisters, Kewalram learned the delicate balance between work and play, discipline and freedom. Little did he know that these carefree days of flying kites and playing Gilli-danda were the foundation of a journey that would take him far beyond the dusty streets of Sehwan, leading him to become one of the most influential figures in India's oil history.

One evening, as the setting sun cast a golden hue over their home, Kewalram sat under the shade of a neem tree with his father.

"Baba," Kewalram asked, his young voice full of curiosity, "why do you work so hard all the time?"

Boolchand smiled softly, stroking his beard. "Because, beta, it's my duty to take care of this family. Your amma and I want to give you and your sisters the best we can."

"But you always look tired," Kewalram said, his brow furrowed in concern.

Boolchand smiled. "That's just part of life. Hard work is what makes a man, Kewalram. One day, you'll understand when you have your own responsibilities."

Kewalram was quiet for a moment, then asked, "Will I have to work like you?"

"You will work, but you'll find your own path," Boolchand replied. "And who knows, maybe you'll do something far greater than I ever could."

Kewalram's eyes shone with curiosity. "Greater? Like what?"

"Like building something important... something that helps people," Boolchand said, his voice filled with quiet conviction.

The boy nodded, though he didn't fully understand. He simply knew that his father believed in him, and that, for now, was enough.

As Kewalram grew older, the family's financial struggles became more apparent. His father's income as a clerk could only stretch so far, and with two daughters nearing marriageable age, there was constant talk of dowries and expenses. One evening, Kewalram overheard his parents talking in hushed tones.

"Asudi, we've saved every rupee we can, but it's not enough for both the girls' marriages and Kewal's education," Boolchand said, worry lacing his voice.

Asudi sighed, wiping her hands on her apron. "I know, but Kewal is smart. He could do something extraordinary if we help him study."

Kewalram, standing just outside the door, clenched his fists. He didn't want to be a burden. He wanted to help.

The next day, he approached his mother. "Amma, I want to give tuitions."

Asudi looked at him in surprise. "Tuitions? But you're just a boy."

"I'm good at math, and the other children in town... they could use help. I can earn money for my own education."

Her eyes softened as she knelt down in front of him. "You're still so young, Kewal."

"I may be young, but I can help," he said firmly.

Asudi smiled, cupping his face in her hands. "You've always been different, haven't you?"

From that day onward, Kewalram began tutoring younger children in mathematics, earning a small sum that he saved diligently for his future education. Every evening after his lessons, he would sit under the neem tree with a pile of books, scribbling numbers, lost in the world of algebra and equations.

Kewalram's mother, however, grew concerned about the unsavoury influences prevalent in Sehwan, where they resided at the time. Determined to provide a better environment for her son, she decided to send him to Rohri to live with her brother, who worked in the railway service there. At Khiaram's school in Rohri, Kewalram thrived in the new environment. During his one-year stay, he quickly became popular both within the school and the railway colony. His natural leadership qualities shone through as he took charge of his group of friends, excelling in both academics and sports.

A particularly memorable aspect of his time in Rohri was the formation of a small theatrical group within the railway colony. Together, they staged dramas in verandas and courtyards, drawing enthusiastic audiences. Among his friends was a talented singer who always performed female roles—a necessity in those days when no society girl would act alongside boys.

The Kanuga family relocated to Sukkur when Kewalram's father secured a position there. Sukkur, with its vibrant streets and the flowing Indus River, became the backdrop of his formative years. He enrolled in the Tilak Municipal High School, a place where his journey as a bright and determined student truly began. Kewalram's academic achievements soon became the talk of the town when he matriculated, becoming the first in the Kanuga family to pass the challenging examination on the first attempt. In those days, the matriculation examination was regarded as one of the most formidable hurdles, making Kewalram's success all the more significant.

At Tilak Municipal High School, Kewalram wasn't just a stellar student; he was a trusted leader among his peers. Excelling in cricket, football, and volleyball, he earned the nickname "Penalty Saver" for his remarkable skills as a goalkeeper. His talent on the field mirrored his resilience and focus in academics. Despite his prowess in most subjects, drawing proved to be his Achilles' heel. Mr. Jhamandas, the drawing teacher, made tireless efforts to spark an interest in the subject, but Kewalram's aversion to it remained steadfast. Each year during the annual examinations, he faced the nerve-wracking challenge of securing just enough marks to pass in drawing. Fortunately, the subject didn't influence overall rankings, sparing him from any major setbacks.

Beyond academics and sports, Kewalram served as the class monitor, a role that often placed him in challenging situations. On one occasion, while substituting for an absent teacher, he faced disruptive behaviour from a fellow student—ironically, the son of a prominent advocate in Sukkur. Despite repeated warnings, the boy continued to misbehave, prompting Kewalram to take decisive action. He physically escorted the boy out of the classroom, an act that led to a confrontation with the boy's influential father the next day. The matter escalated to the headmaster, but Kewalram's integrity and the support of his teachers prevailed. The headmaster and class teacher stood firmly by him, emphasizing that the boy's conduct had long been problematic. Remarkably, the incident ended amicably, with the boy offering a written apology and eventually becoming one of Kewalram's close friends. This episode instilled in Kewalram a lifelong lesson in firmness and fairness, traits that would serve him well in his illustrious career.

These early experiences in Sukkur shaped Kewalram's character, laying the foundation for the visionary leader he would later become. His journey from the corridors of Tilak Municipal High School to the oil fields of Assam was marked by resilience, a commitment to excellence, and an unwavering belief in the power of education and discipline.

Chapter 2:
The College Years (1930-1935)

The bustling streets of Karachi were a stark contrast to the quiet town of Sehwan. Kewalram, now a young man of eighteen, stood at the gates of Dayaram Jethmal Sindh College, feeling both nervous and excited. The college's grand entrance before him symbolized the opportunity and future he had fought hard to reach. Taking a deep breath, he stepped inside.

Within weeks, Kewalram had already distinguished himself in his classes. His professors quickly noticed his keen intellect, especially in physics and mathematics. But what truly set him apart was his relentless thirst for knowledge. He approached his studies with a singular focus, aware of the heavy responsibility that came with the privilege of education. His family's financial situation had always been precarious, and he knew that every rupee spent on his education was an investment in their collective future.

One afternoon, Kewalram sat under the shade of a banyan tree on campus, surrounded by a group of friends. His close friend, Ratanlal, nudged him playfully.

"Kewalram, you're always buried in your books," Ratanlal teased. "Don't you ever take a break?"

Kewalram grinned without looking up from his notebook. "Solving problems is how I relax. Isn't that normal?"

Ratanlal rolled his eyes. "Normal? Not really. Impressive? Definitely."

The group laughed, but Kewalram remained focused. College, for him, wasn't just an opportunity—it was a lifeline. His success here would determine not only his future but also his family's well-being.

Back in Sehwan, traditions ran deep. Families often negotiated dowries to secure advantageous marriages for their daughters, and Kewalram's academic brilliance made him a highly sought-after groom. Among those vying for his hand was a wealthy zamindar, the father of Ganga. The zamindar's offer was the most generous, promising Rs 1000 in dowry if Kewalram agreed to marry his daughter.

One evening, Kewalram's father, Boolchand, entered the room with a thoughtful expression.

"Kewal," he began, sitting beside his son, "we've received an offer."

Kewalram looked up, curious. "What kind of offer, Baba?"

"The zamindar from Sehwan is offering Rs 1000 if you marry his daughter, Ganga," Boolchand explained. "He's willing to give Rs 500 in advance, which could cover your college fees."

Kewalram's heart raced. Marriage wasn't something he had considered—his mind was entirely focused on his studies. But the practicality of the offer was undeniable.

"Do you think this is the right decision?" Kewalram asked, his voice uncertain.

Boolchand placed a hand on his son's shoulder. "In our world, we make the best of the opportunities we're given. This isn't just about marriage—it's about securing your future. With this advance, you can continue your education without worry."

Kewalram sat in silence, weighing the situation. He knew how much his education meant to him. But realizing that dream through a dowry felt strange. Yet, in the practical world they lived in, this was a lifeline—an opportunity too significant to ignore.

After a moment, he nodded. "If this is what it takes, Baba, then I'll do it."

With that decision, Kewalram's life took a new turn. The Rs 500 advance wasn't just money—it was the gateway to the education that would shape his destiny. He soon enrolled in D.J. Sindh College, leaving the traditions of Sehwan behind as he embraced the opportunities of the academic world.

One evening, as Kewalram walked home from college, he noticed a small group of men gathered around a street corner. Curious, he approached them.

"What's happening?" he asked, peering over someone's shoulder.

"They're talking about the Salt Satyagraha," a young man replied. "Gandhiji's call to defy the British salt laws."

Kewalram's heart quickened. He had read about the movement in the newspapers, but here, on the streets of Karachi, it felt more real. As the speakers talked about civil disobedience, standing up against colonial oppression, and the fight for India's independence, something stirred inside him.

That night, Kewalram couldn't sleep. He tossed and turned, his mind racing with thoughts of joining the movement. Finally, as the first light of dawn crept through the window, he made his decision.

The next day, he approached his father. "Baba, I want to participate in the Salt Satyagraha."

Boolchand looked at him, startled. "You want to join the independence movement?"

"Yes," Kewalram said, his voice steady. "I can't sit by while our country suffers under British rule."

Boolchand sighed deeply, rubbing his temples. "Son, I admire your passion. But think of your education. You've worked so hard to get here. You could be thrown in jail. What will happen to your future then?"

Kewalram's gaze was resolute. "My future is tied to this country's freedom. If we don't stand up now, when will we?"

For a moment, Boolchand said nothing. Finally, he nodded slowly. "You're your own man now, Kewalram. If this is what you believe in, I won't stop you."

Kewalram joined the local chapter of the Salt Satyagraha movement, attending meetings, distributing leaflets, and participating in peaceful protests. The thrill of being part of something larger than himself filled him with purpose. But it wasn't long before the consequences of defying British rule caught up with him.

One afternoon, while leading a group of students in a peaceful march, they were stopped by British police officers.

"Disperse at once!" one of the officers barked.

Kewalram stepped forward. "We are protesting peacefully. We have the right to speak against injustice."

Without warning, the officer struck Kewalram with his baton. The blow landed hard on his shoulder, but he stood firm, his jaw clenched in defiance. The other students watched in stunned silence as the officers pushed them back, arresting several of the leaders, including Kewalram.

As he was hauled away, Kewalram's thoughts were not on the pain in his shoulder, but on the future of his country.

After a few days in police lock up, Kewalram was released, his spirit unbroken. However, his father's warnings weighed on him. He realized that while his heart burned for India's freedom, he also had a duty to his family and his future. With a heavy heart, he stepped back from active participation in the movement and returned to his studies.

The years passed in a whirlwind of equations, late-night study sessions, and exams. By 1933, Kewalram had graduated with a degree in Physics, and his reputation as a mathematical prodigy had only grown.

His professors often spoke of his potential for a bright future in academia, but life, as it often does, had other plans.

During these college years, Kewalram discovered a new passion—writing. His love for algebra and mathematics inspired him to author books on the subject. By his final year, he had written two books on algebra, not just filled with dry formulas, but designed to simplify complex concepts for students. He wanted to make the subject approachable, breaking down its complexities into understandable basics.

One evening in the college library, his friend Jitender Singh sat beside him, flipping through the pages of one of Kewalram's manuscripts.

"You've done something remarkable here," Jitender said, scanning the carefully written equations and explanations. "This could really help students struggling with algebra."

Kewalram smiled, a flicker of pride lighting his face. "I just wanted to make it easier for them. Algebra doesn't have to be something to fear—it's all about mastering the fundamentals."

Jitender grinned. "Mark my words, this book will change how students learn."

Kewalram had no idea how prophetic those words would be. Years later, one of the books he had written during his college days would become a part of the school curriculum for matriculation students across the region. His work was a testament to both his deep understanding of mathematics and his passion for teaching others. It was a legacy that would continue to inspire future generations of students, long after his college days were over.

In 1935, life took a new turn for Kewalram, one he hadn't anticipated to come so soon. His parents had fixed the dater of his marriage to Ganga, the daughter of a wealthy Zamindar. The decision had been made long ago, but now the day had arrived.

All these years, the topic of marriage loomed in the background. Kewalram's mother and the girl's parents were eager to see the match finalized. However, Kewalram managed to postpone the matter while he focused on his education. Following his successful completion of the B.Sc. examination and securing a teaching position at Hyderabad High School—a prestigious institution originally a government school, the pressure to marry became unavoidable.

Finally, the marriage took place on March 31, 1935, marking a significant milestone in his personal life. Yet, this joyous occasion was overshadowed by a profound sorrow, as Kewalram's mother passed away just days before the wedding. Such is the unpredictable nature of destiny.

As Kewalram stood beside Ganga during the rituals, he glanced at her. She looked serene, her eyes lowered, focused on the priest's chants. His mind, however, wandered. The wealth her father had—while impressive—meant little to him. What truly mattered, Kewalram thought, was creating something meaningful together, building a life that would stand the test of time.

After the wedding, Ganga joined Kewalram in Karachi, a city that was bustling with life and opportunity. The busy streets, vibrant markets, and distant smell of the sea made Karachi feel like a world away from the small, quiet town of Sehwan.

One evening, as they walked hand in hand through the crowded streets, Ganga looked around in awe. "Karachi is so different from Sehwan," she said softly, her eyes scanning the brightly lit shops and the fast-moving crowds. "Do you think we'll make it here, Kanuga ji?"

Kewalram smiled and squeezed her hand gently. "We will, Ganga," he said, his voice filled with quiet determination. "It's all about adjusting, isn't it? And together, we'll build a happy life here."

Ganga nodded, her initial hesitation slowly melting away as she drew comfort from his confidence. The city was overwhelming, but with Kewalram by her side, she felt a growing sense of hope.

A year later, their lives changed forever when they welcomed their first child, a daughter named Mira. Ganga cradled the tiny baby in her arms, her heart swelling with joy. "She's perfect" she whispered, gazing at Mira's peaceful face.

Kewalram beamed with pride. "She's our future," he said softly. "She will bring a lot of luck to our family."

Chapter 3:
Into the Oil Fields (1935-1947)

The vibrant city of Karachi slowly became home for Kewalram and Ganga. After their wedding, life settled into a steady rhythm. Kewalram had secured a teaching position at prestigious Sadhu T. L. Vaswani's Meera Education Trust, where he taught mathematics to eager young minds, inspiring hope in the future of their nation.

One evening, as Ganga placed a cup of tea in front of him, her soft smile reflected the warmth they had built together. "You seem happy teaching," she remarked gently.

Kewalram looked up from the papers he was grading, the weariness in his eyes replaced by a smile. "I am," he admitted. "But I feel like there's something more I need to do—something bigger."

Ganga, ever the wise companion, sat beside him, her eyes filled with understanding. "You've always had that fire within you, Kanuga ji. You're not meant for small things."

He smiled softly, taking her hand. "Maybe. But for now, this job is good. It gives us a start, and that's enough for the moment."

Life was good, steady, and fulfilling. During this time, their family grew as they welcomed their second daughter, Kaushalya, into the world. However, the path life had laid out for Kewalram was about to take an unexpected turn.

One afternoon, as Kewalram was wrapping up his class, a man in a sharp, tailored suit entered the school. His air of authority was unmistakable as he scanned the room with mild disinterest.

"Kewalram Kanuga?" the man asked.

"Yes, that's me," Kewalram replied, dusting chalk from his hands.

The man straightened his tie, his demeanor businesslike. "I'm Mr. Turner from Burmah Oil Company. We've heard you have a sharp mind for numbers. We need someone who can handle complex calculations and logistics at our Karachi office. Are you interested?"

Kewalram blinked, surprised by the offer. "Burmah Oil? The British company?"

Turner smirked. "Indeed. If you prove yourself, there's room for growth. We have operations across India, even in Rangoon."

That evening, Kewalram discussed the offer with Ganga. Her eyes widened in surprise.

"Burmah Oil? That's a big company," she said, her tone cautious. "But it's British. Do you really want to work for them Kanuga ji?"

Kewalram sighed, running a hand through his hair. "I've thought about that. But if I join, I could learn things—things that could help our country someday. The oil industry is crucial for India's future."

Ganga nodded slowly, her trust in him unwavering. "If you feel it's the right step, I'll stand by you."

With Ganga's support, Kewalram decided to join Burmah Oil. It wasn't just a job—it was an opportunity to learn, to grow, and perhaps, one day, to make a difference.

The first few months were intense. Kewalram worked long hours as a clerk in the logistics department, calculating supply routes, managing shipments, and overseeing operations. His dedication quickly caught the eye of his superiors.

One evening, while Kewalram was poring over maps of oil fields, his manager, Mr. Fleming, entered the room, a cigarette dangling from his lips.

"You've got a sharp head, Kanuga," Fleming remarked, glancing out the window. "But there's more to this business than just numbers."

Kewalram looked up, intrigued. "What do you mean?"

Fleming exhaled a cloud of smoke. "Oil isn't just about drilling and selling. It's about power. Control. The British Empire runs on oil, and whoever controls it controls the game."

The weight of Fleming' words settled heavily on Kewalram. Oil wasn't merely a commodity—it was the lifeblood of empires. As an Indian working for the British, he found himself torn between loyalty to his work and the future of his homeland.

By 1939, Kewalram had proven his worth. His hard work led to assignments in Digboi, Assam, and even Rangoon. These trips were eye-opening, revealing the vastness of the oil industry and the glaring inequalities between the British and their Indian subordinates.

One evening in Rangoon, after a grueling day, Kewalram sat with a few Indian colleagues at a small tea shop. The air was thick with frustration, and Mahendra, one of his coworkers, voiced what they all felt.

"They think we're 'Kala Sahibs'—black gentlemen," Mahendra said bitterly. "No matter how hard we work, we'll never be equals."

Kewalram frowned but didn't argue. He, too, had seen the disparities. Yet, deep down, he believed that change was coming. The winds of freedom were beginning to stir, even if it wasn't immediately visible.

As the years passed, Kewalram didn't just gain technical knowledge—he learned the art of negotiation, diplomacy, and leadership. He watched the British closely, learning from their strategies and preparing for the day when India would stand on its own.

During this time, Kewalram and Ganga welcomed two more children—Nandlal and Giridharilal—into their growing family. Their personal lives intertwined with the rapidly evolving political landscape of India and the shifting fortunes of the oil industry.

In 1947, when India's long-awaited independence was announced, the joy was overshadowed by the harrowing reality of Partition. For Kewalram, this meant his beloved home in Karachi was now part of Pakistan. The country was no longer his, and the future was uncertain.

One evening, Ganga sat on the edge of their bed, folding clothes with trembling hands. Her face was pale, tears brimming in her eyes.

"I never thought we'd have to leave everything behind," she whispered, her voice shaking.

Kewalram knelt beside her, placing a comforting hand on her shoulder. "I know, Ganga," he said softly. "But we'll make a new life. We've done it before, and we'll do it again."

She looked at him, searching for reassurance. "But where will we go Kanuga ji?" she asked, her voice a mere whisper.

"Maybe Digboi," Kewalram answered, his tone resolute. "I've heard the company is planning to transfer me there. It's far, but we'll manage."

Ganga wiped her tears, her voice gaining strength. "As long as we're together, we'll be fine."

Partition had taken much—their home, their city, the life they had built. But it also marked the beginning of a new chapter. After crossing the border, they found temporary refuge in Gujarat, staying in a camp for a few months before rebuilding their lives in a new, independent India.

Once again, they would start over—together.

In 1948, Kewalram's life took yet another unexpected turn. He was selected for a prestigious six-month training program in the UK—a rare and invaluable opportunity. Yet the timing couldn't have been worse. Ganga was pregnant again, already caring for their two daughters and two sons, all while living in a Sindhi refugee camp in

Anand, Gujarat. Her parents, also displaced by Partition, shared the crowded and challenging conditions of the camp. The thought of leaving her in such a vulnerable state weighed heavily on Kewalram's heart.

As his departure day neared, Kewalram sat beside Ganga on their modest bed in the camp. The night air was thick with unspoken worries.

"I hate leaving you now," he confessed, gripping her hand. "Especially with everything going on."

Ganga, though worn and burdened, managed a faint smile, her resilience shining through. "You must go Kanuga ji," she urged gently. "This opportunity is too important—for us, for the children. I'll manage." But the strain in her voice betrayed her struggle.

Kewalram sighed deeply. "I'll write to you every week. Once I'm back, things will be better. We'll make a fresh start."

The day of his departure came with mixed emotions. As Kewalram left for London, the weight of his responsibilities tugged at him. He was traveling on a Pakistani travel permit due to the short notice, as his Indian passport hadn't been processed yet—a decision that would later prove perilous. Despite the uncertainties, Kewalram focused on the opportunities ahead: the chance to gain new knowledge, build connections, and face unforeseen challenges.

Once in London, Kewalram's world changed dramatically. The training was rigorous but deeply fulfilling. More than the technical lessons, he forged key relationships with senior managers in the head office, such as Rupert Carey and William Maclachlan. But the most significant friendship that blossomed during this time was with the renowned geologist, Percy Evans.

Their first meeting, however, was far from promising. It was at the International Geologists Conference where Evans, known for his sharp wit and high standards, was unimpressed to learn that Kewalram only held a BSc in Physics.

"I'm sorry, Mr Kanuga," Evans said, raising an eyebrow, "but this conference is for geologists. You might find yourself out of your place here."

The sting of rejection was sharp, but Kewalram didn't argue. Instead, he doubled down. Over the following weeks, he immersed himself in the study of geology, self-tutoring and observing the work of experts with an unrelenting curiosity. Always a quick learner, his efforts soon caught Evans' attention.

During a field demonstration, Evans noticed Kewalram's insightful questions and his keen interest in the work. "You've been doing your homework," Evans remarked with a smile. His initial skepticism had turned to respect. "Maybe you're not so out of place after all."

From that moment, their relationship flourished. Kewalram became part of Evans' inner circle, a connection that would prove invaluable in the years to come—especially when oil was discovered in Naharkatiya. Evans' support lent Kewalram credibility and confidence, key factors when the Government of India and Burmah Oil joined forces to form Oil India Ltd.

But Kewalram's time in the UK wasn't without its difficulties. One morning, as he skimmed through the headlines of a London newspaper, his blood ran cold. The words leaped off the page: Arrest and Deportation Order Issued. His Pakistani travel permit had caught the attention of the authorities, and they were threatening to deport him.

"What do I do now?" he muttered, pacing his small apartment. Panic surged through him. If he were deported, it could destroy everything.

Fortunately, his company stepped in. After intense negotiations with the British authorities, they secured him a temporary British passport, leveraging the fact that India and Pakistan were still part of the British Commonwealth. The ordeal served as a stark reminder of the delicate nature of his situation.

After six long months, Kewalram returned to India, changed in more ways than he could have imagined. He had gained not only knowledge but also newfound confidence and connections that would shape the rest of his career. His first act upon returning was to exchange the temporary British passport for an Indian one, a gesture that symbolized both his personal commitment and the official recognition of his and his family's status as Indian citizens.

However, the challenges didn't stop there. One evening, as Kewalram sat at the kitchen table, deep in thought, Ganga joined him, holding their youngest child, Leelawanti, born shortly after his return.

"They denied the compensatory land, didn't they?" Ganga asked softly, her voice laced with concern.

Kewalram sighed, glancing at the rejection letter in his hands. "Yes," he said, his voice heavy. "Because we didn't cross into India during Partition, we're not eligible for land compensation." He paused, watching their children play nearby. "Others are rebuilding their lives with that land, but we'll have to find another way."

Ganga, exhausted but resolute, sat beside him. "Do you think we'll ever get back what we lost, Kanuga ji?" she asked, her voice trembling with both hope and fear.

Kewalram gently took her hand, giving it a reassuring squeeze. "Maybe not in the way others have," he said, gazing at their children. "But we have something better. I still have my job, and with it, we'll rebuild. It may be slow, but we'll get there."

Though the denial of compensation stung, they found solace in the stability Kewalram's job provided. With the knowledge and skills, he had gained in the UK, Kewalram's career was on an upward trajectory. He had risen from clerical work to overseeing operations, his responsibilities growing with each new task.

One evening, as they sat together after dinner, Ganga observed, "You're different now. You've changed."

Kewalram smiled, reflecting on his journey. "I've learned a lot," he admitted. "I'm not the same man who left six months ago. I know more, and I've met people who believe in me. I have made friendship with Percy Evans, the man who is called as the father of Assam's geology".

That friendship proved pivotal, especially when oil was discovered in Assam. Evans' influence opened many doors for Kewalram, and before long, his career was soaring. He soon moved from operational roles to overseeing refinery and distribution functions.

A major turning point came when an Englishman, originally appointed as General Manager in Digboi, declined to relocate to India.

"They want me to take over as Acting General Manager," Kewalram told Ganga one evening, disbelief still evident in his voice. "Can you imagine that?"

"Why wouldn't they?" Ganga smiled proudly. "You've earned it."

Kewalram's rise within Burmah Oil was a testament to his hard work, resilience, and the relationships he had cultivated along the way. His friendship with Percy Evans had become legendary.

Despite all the hardships and losses, Kewalram's journey had come full circle. He had left India uncertain and burdened with fear but returned stronger, wiser, and ready for whatever lay ahead. Though their challenges were far from over, Kewalram and Ganga faced them with renewed strength and hope—together.

Chapter 4:
Digboi Days (1948–1957)

With heavy hearts and weary souls, Kewalram, Ganga, and their five children boarded the crowded train departing from the refugee camp in Anand. The platform buzzed with the noise of families in transit—some filled with hope, others consumed by uncertainty. As the train jolted forward, Kewalram leaned his head against the window, watching the unfamiliar landscape blur by. Yet, his mind wandered far ahead, tangled in thoughts of the uncertain journey they had begun.

Ganga, noticing the deep lines of worry etched on her husband's face, shifted their youngest child in her lap and softly asked, "What weighs on your mind, Kanuga ji?"

He sighed, his gaze still fixed on the passing fields. "Calcutta, Gauhati... then Digboi," he murmured. "So many unknowns, Ganga. I don't know what awaits us."

Ganga placed a reassuring hand on his arm, her voice steady. "We've come this far, Kanuga ji. We'll make it through. We always have."

The train rattled on, its rhythmic clatter a constant reminder of the long journey ahead. From broad gauge to meter gauge, the family switched trains at countless stations, each stop blurring into the next. The children, restless and exhausted, struggled to sleep on the hard benches, frequently jolted awake by the train's rough movements. Kewalram and Ganga remained vigilant, their hearts heavy with the weight of the journey and the constant harassment by Pakistani police at the borders.

As the train wound its way through East Pakistan, crossing borders and rivers, they endured sleepless nights and endless challenges. A ferry crossing only added to their exhaustion, with uncertainty gnawing at them mile after mile. Yet, there was no turning back.

Finally, after what felt like a lifetime, the train's shrill whistle pierced the stillness of the night as they arrived in Digboi. It was the middle of the night, and the small, isolated platform was bathed in dim light. The scent of oil filled the air, mingling with the earthy aroma of Assam's dense forests. The place was a stark contrast to the bustling, sun-soaked streets of Karachi they had left behind.

"This is it," Kewalram said quietly, his eyes scanning the empty station and the distant oil fields. Despite the loneliness of the night, he felt a small stir of hope.

Ganga pulled her shawl tighter around her shoulders, her gaze sweeping across the unfamiliar landscape. "It feels like a world away from everything we knew," she whispered, her voice tinged with both awe and trepidation.

Kewalram took her hand in his, his grip firm with quiet resolve. "It is," he replied softly. "But this place is growing, Ganga. There's more here than just oil and gas. We'll rebuild our life—brick by brick. Together."

She looked into his eyes, her own softening with the same determination that had carried them through years of struggle. In the stillness of that moment, standing on the brink of a new beginning, they knew they would face whatever came next—side by side, ready to rebuild their world in this strange, oil-soaked land.

The company allotted Kewalram one of the heritage bungalows—a symbol of status and tradition in the oil town. The bungalow, perched on a gentle hillock, stood out with its distinct British architectural style, a reminder of the colonial past that had shaped much of Digboi's identity.

As Kewalram stepped out of the car and onto the gravel driveway, he paused to take in the sight before him. Like many homes in Digboi, the bungalow was raised on stilts—a practical design that allowed cool air to circulate beneath, keeping the interiors cooler during the hot Assam summers. The sloping roof, wide verandas, and tall windows exuded an old-world charm, hallmarks of British architecture.

Ganga stood beside him, her eyes following the curve of the large wrap-around veranda that seemed to beckon the cool breeze from the nearby tea gardens. "It's beautiful," she whispered, as if the serenity of the place demanded silence.

Kewalram smiled. "It has character, doesn't it?"

They walked up the wooden steps, which creaked slightly, adding to the bungalow's lived-in warmth. Inside, the spacious interiors unfolded before them—high ceilings with exposed wooden beams, polished teak floors gleaming in the afternoon sun, and rooms that seemed to breathe with history. Simple yet elegant colonial-era fixtures adorned the walls, offering a stark contrast to the lush greenery framed by every window.

The most striking feature of the bungalow was the wide veranda that wrapped around the front and sides. From there, Kewalram could gaze at the rolling hills and tea gardens stretching far into the horizon. The garden was a riot of color—bougainvillea, hibiscus, and orchids bloomed in abundance, tended by generations of caretakers who had worked these estates long before Kewalram's arrival.

As they wandered from room to room, Kewalram felt the bungalow's history in every corner. It was more than just a house—it was a relic of a time when the British ruled these lands and controlled Assam's vast oil resources. The dining room, with its long table and high-backed chairs, seemed ready for evening parties where tales of oil exploration and life in the tea gardens would have been shared over glasses of whiskey and gin.

"The view from the bedroom," Ganga called, her voice echoing down the hallway. Kewalram followed her voice into the master bedroom, which opened onto a private balcony overlooking a dense patch of forest. "It's like we're living in a different world," she said, her eyes reflecting the tranquillity of their new home.

Kewalram nodded, recognizing the deeper significance of their new residence. The bungalow wasn't just a place to live; it was a symbol of his rising stature within the company. As he stood in the doorway, gazing out at the peaceful surroundings, he couldn't help but reflect on the long journey that had brought him here—from his humble beginnings in Karachi to this colonial relic in Assam's oil belt.

The next day, Kewalram reported to the Assam Oil Company's Digboi office, where he was greeted by Anthony Gowan, a senior manager and an old acquaintance.

"Mr. KB Kanuga! Welcome to Digboi," Gowan said, shaking his hand warmly. "We're glad to have you here. There's plenty of exciting work ahead."

Kanuga smiled, though the weight of Partition and the upheaval of their move still weighed on him. "I'm ready to contribute in any way I can," he replied earnestly.

"With your sharp mind, I have no doubt you'll make an impact," Gowan said, his grin widening. "I'll be counting on you, KB."

From that day forward, Gowan referred to him simply as "KB"—a term of camaraderie that marked the start of their partnership.

Kanuga threw himself into learning the intricacies of oil production. Digboi's refinery, one of the oldest in the world, was a marvel of industry, but its operations were complex, requiring a deep understanding of both technical and logistical details. Eager to immerse himself in the work, Kanuga quickly grasped the nuances of drilling and refining.

In the weeks that followed, Kewalram and Ganga set about transforming the heritage bungalow into their home. Though it felt empty at first, with each item they unpacked, warmth began to fill the old walls. Ganga thoughtfully arranged their few belongings, while the children explored every corner, turning the vast living room into their playground.

"Feels like a real home now," Ganga said one evening as she adjusted a framed photo on the mantelpiece.

Kewalram smiled. "It does. But it's not just the things we brought. It's the life we're building here."

Their bungalow quickly became a gathering place for colleagues and friends. The large living room often filled with lively discussions about the challenges of oil exploration and the political changes sweeping through post-independence India.

One evening, after a particularly long day at work, Kewalram sat on the veranda with a cup of tea, his eyes scanning the horizon. "It's strange, isn't it?" he mused to Ganga, who had joined him. "Hearing the oil rig machinery hum in the distance, knowing we're part of something so much bigger."

Ganga, cradling her own cup, nodded. "Bigger than us, yes," she agreed. "But also, this... it's ours now. The British built these homes, but we're the ones living in them, shaping the future."

Kewalram nodded, thoughtful. "This bungalow, this whole place—it's part of a legacy. A colonial one. But we're making it ours."

As the sun dipped below the horizon, casting the sky in hues of orange and purple, Kewalram leaned back in his chair, a deep sense of purpose settling over him. "We're part of Digboi's history now, Ganga," he said softly. "And we'll be part of its future too."

Their quiet evenings on the veranda became a cherished ritual, a time to reflect on their journey, their growing family, and the new life they were building. It was in this very bungalow, in 1950, that their sixth child, Lakshman, was born—ushering in a new chapter in their unfolding story.

The early years of K B Kanuga's career were marked by a deep connection to the town of Digboi, the birthplace of the oil industry in

India. But his contributions to this historic town extended far beyond the oil fields. Kanuga was not only a brilliant oilman but also a man who believed in the power of culture and community. His involvement in promoting Indian culture and literature in Digboi was as significant as his role in shaping the country's oil industry.

As the family grew, Kewalram and Ganga found themselves at the centre of a bustling household. Their three daughters and three sons filled their days with laughter, chatter, and the occasional squabble. Evenings were their favourite time—a chance to unwind together after the long hours of work and school. After dinner, when the house was finally quiet, Kewalram would suggest, "How about a drive?"

This post-dinner ritual had become a cherished routine. The entire family—Kewalram, Ganga, and their six children—would pile into their trusty old Studebaker Commander. It was always a tight fit, with everyone packed closely together in the car, but that was part of the charm. Ganga, sitting in the front seat, would often laugh and say, "It's delightfully crowded, but somehow, it's just right."

Kewalram would steer the car through the sprawling oil fields of Digboi, the headlights cutting through the evening mist. The children would gaze out the windows, pointing out the flickering oil rigs in the distance. "Look, Baba! The fields seem endless tonight!" one of his sons would exclaim, his face pressed against the glass.

Their favorite destination was the Margherita bridge. It had become a tradition to drive up to the bridge, stop for a while, and just enjoy the cool night air. Ganga would sit quietly, taking in the view, while Kewalram shared stories with the kids about the early days in Digboi. "This town," he would say, his voice filled with pride, "was the place where oil was discovered in India. One day, you'll all understand how much this place is important to our country."

Over the years, the family outgrew the old Studebaker, and Kewalram upgraded to a more spacious DeSoto. "This one's got more room," he'd say with a grin as the kids excitedly climbed in. The DeSoto quickly became as beloved as their old car, and the post-dinner drives continued, the family now a little less cramped but still packed with the same warmth and joy.

Even after years later, the DeSoto held onto its original charm. It had been refurbished with an Audi engine to keep it running smoothly, but it still retained its classic look—the Digboi look, as Kewalram liked to call it. The leather seats, worn from use, remained just as they were, a comforting reminder of the countless drives they had shared as a family.

One evening, as they reached the Margherita bridge, Kewalram turned to Ganga with a smile. "It's funny," he said, patting the dashboard, "this car has seen us through so much. And yet, no matter how much we upgrade it, it still feels like home."

Ganga, her hand resting on his, nodded. "It's not just the car. It's us, all of us, together."

Their children, now older, sat in the back, smiling as they listened to their parents. For them, these drives weren't just about seeing the oil fields or the bridge—they were about being a family, squeezed into a car that carried the weight of their shared history.

As they drove back toward Digboi that night, Kewalram glanced at the rearview mirror, catching the reflection of his children, their faces bathed in the soft glow of the car's lights. The old DeSoto hummed along, a part of the landscape as much as the oil fields and the roads they travelled on.

In 1950, Kewalram Kanuga was elected the President of the prestigious Digboi India Club, a position that held great significance in the region. The club, established in 1918, was more than just a place for social gatherings—it had become a hub for promoting Indian culture, literature, and sports at a time when British influence still loomed over many aspects of life. Kanuga understood the importance of this institution for the Indian community in Digboi.

One evening, as he sat with Ganga in their modest Digboi home, he spoke of his vision for the club. "The Digboi India Club is a platform for us, for Indians," he began, his voice filled with determination. "It's where we can come together to celebrate who we are—our culture, our literature, our sports. It's not just a club; it's a symbol of our identity."

Ganga looked at him thoughtfully. "And you, as president, have the chance to make it something even greater," she said, encouraging him.

Kanuga nodded, his eyes bright with ambition. "Yes. I want it to be a place where writers, thinkers, and sports enthusiasts can thrive. A place where people can come together, despite all the barriers that exist."

Under his leadership, the club flourished. It became a beacon of cultural pride, a place where Indians in Digboi could express themselves freely, engage in intellectual discussions, and celebrate their heritage. Kanuga's passion for fostering unity and pride in Indian identity was reflected in every event and gathering held at the club during his presidency.

But Kanuga's commitment to culture didn't stop there. A decade later, in 1960, he played a pivotal role in establishing the Ramleela Coordination Committee in Digboi. One evening, during a discussion with some of the town's prominent figures, Kanuga brought up the idea.

"We need to ensure that our traditions are preserved," he said earnestly. "The Ramleela is an important part of our culture, especially for the Hindi-speaking community here. If we don't organize it properly, it could fade away."

One of his colleagues, nodding in agreement, asked, "So what do you propose?"

Kanuga leaned forward, his voice full of conviction. "We form a committee. A Ramleela Coordination Committee to organize the annual event, to make sure it thrives for generations to come."

The others looked at him, impressed by his dedication. "And you, Kanuga Saheb, should lead it," one of them said.

Kanuga accepted the responsibility with humility. The Ramleela, a traditional theatrical representation of the Ramayana, became a unifying event for the people of Digboi under his leadership. It transcended religious and linguistic boundaries, bringing the community together in a celebration of shared heritage.

As the festival grew in popularity, Kanuga often stood on the sidelines, watching the vibrant performances with a satisfied smile. "This," he would say to Ganga, "is what makes all the effort worth it—seeing our culture alive, seeing people come together like this."

His efforts in organizing such events reflected his deep-rooted belief that cultural heritage was just as important as oil in building a strong community. The Digboi India Club and the Ramleela Coordination Committee stood as lasting legacies of Kanuga's early years in Digboi, showcasing his dedication not only to professional excellence but also to cultural leadership.

In addition to his contributions to the oil industry and the cultural life of Digboi, Kewalram Kanuga was deeply committed to the spirit of service and community development. His leadership extended beyond the workplace, and in 1952, inspired by his membership of the Lions Club of Calcutta, he took a bold step in forming the Lions Club of Digboi.

It was a quiet evening in Digboi, and as Kewalram sat on the veranda of his bungalow, sipping tea, he turned to Ganga with a thoughtful look.

"You know," he began, "Our company has built so much here—homes, hospital, school, sports facilities, a community—but there's something more we can do for the people beyond these oil fields. The rural belt around us, places like Bogapani, Tingrai, and Makum—they've been largely neglected. The tea planters and district officials rarely address their needs."

Ganga looked at him, understanding where his mind was headed. "You're thinking about the starting a group to address their needs, aren't you?"

Kewalram nodded. "Exactly. We need to extend the concept of fellowship through service. The Lions Club of Calcutta showed me how powerful such a group could be. It's not just about socializing—it's about 'We Serve.' That's the motto of the Lions Club. And we can do that here too."

And so, under Kanuga's leadership, the Lions Club of Digboi was born as an offshoot of the Calcutta chapter. It quickly became a beacon of hope and progress for the surrounding rural areas. The club focused on projects that brought real change to communities that had long been overlooked by both the tea planters and the district administration of Lakhimpur, headquartered in Dibrugarh at that time.

The first project they undertook was in Bogapani, a small village not far from the oil fields. The club organized medical camps, providing much-needed healthcare services to the villagers, many of whom had never seen a doctor before. Kanuga personally visited the village with a team of doctors, ensuring that no one was left unattended.

One afternoon, after a long day of setting up the medical camp, one of the villagers, an elderly man with weathered hands, approached Kanuga.

"Saheb, we've never had anyone come to our village like this before," the man said in broken Hindi, his voice filled with gratitude. "You've brought hope to us."

Kanuga smiled, placing a reassuring hand on the man's shoulder. "This is just the beginning. We are here to serve, and we will keep coming back."

The club's work didn't stop at healthcare. Over time, they extended their projects to Tingrai and Makum, focusing on education, sanitation, and livelihood improvement. Schools were built, water wells were dug, and community centres were established, all with the goal of uplifting the rural population.

Kanuga's tireless efforts to bring the Lions Club's mission of service to the region were deeply appreciated by the people of Digboi and the surrounding areas. Under his leadership, the club became a symbol of progress and unity, bridging the gap between the town's oil-driven prosperity and the needs of its neighbouring rural communities.

One evening, during a Lions Club meeting, Bikash, a young engineer, approached Kanuga.

"Sir, I've never seen someone so dedicated to both their profession and their community. You've turned this place into something more than just an oil town."

Kanuga smiled, his eyes twinkling. "It's not about the oil alone, Bikash. It's about the people. Whether it's through industry, sports, or service, we have a duty to give back. We're all connected—whether we realize it or not."

The Lions Club of Digboi thrived under Kewalram's leadership, continuing to serve the rural belt and leaving a lasting impact on the region. His commitment to the motto "We Serve" became a defining aspect of his legacy, showing that true leadership extends beyond business and into the heart of the community.

Kewalram Kanuga knew that beyond the oil fields and the day-to-day operations, communication was key to building a cohesive and engaged community. One evening, while discussing with Ganga over dinner, he mentioned an idea that had been brewing in his mind.

"We've created so much here in Digboi, but we need a way to bring people together, to share stories, updates, and achievements. Something that keeps everyone in the loop, especially as the town grows."

Ganga smiled knowingly. "You're thinking of starting a publication Kanuga ji, aren't you?"

Kewalram nodded. "Exactly. A newsletter—something simple but regular, to capture the essence of life here. We'll call it 'Digboi Batori.'"

And so, with his typical energy and foresight, Kewalram Kanuga initiated the publication of Digboi Batori, a local newsletter that would become the voice of the community. It was printed from a small press near Chari Ali, a bustling area in the heart of Digboi, and quickly became a staple in every household. Through Digboi Batori, the people of Digboi stayed informed about everything, from company news to local events, sports results, and cultural activities.

One morning, as he reviewed the latest edition of the newsletter, Kanuga turned to one of the editors and said, "This is just the beginning. Someday, this will grow into something even larger, something that can reflect not just Digboi, but all of oil exploration activities of Assam."

True to his prediction, Digboi Batori became the precursor to OIL News, which later emerged in Duliajan, capturing the stories and achievements of the broader Oil India community.

But Kewalram's vision for Digboi wasn't limited to news and communication. He had a flair for bringing excitement and cultural vibrancy to the town. The Digboi Club became a hub of activity, hosting not just local events but welcoming celebrities and performers from across India.

One of the most memorable events was the visit of P.C. Sorcar, the famous magician. The club was buzzing with anticipation as the stage was set for Sorcar's performance. That evening, the hall was packed with families, children, and oilmen, all eagerly waiting to be dazzled. As Sorcar performed his tricks, making objects disappear and reappear, the audience gasped and cheered. Kanuga, seated in the front row, couldn't help but smile. "This is what makes a community strong," he whispered to Ganga, "shared moments of wonder and joy."

But the true talk of the town was when the legendary wrestler, Dara Singh, made a detour to visit Digboi. Singh had just finished a much-anticipated bout with his long-time rival, a wrestler from Hungary with the ring name King Kong, in Dibrugarh. The bout had been a sensation, with many from Digboi making the journey to Dibrugarh in company-provided buses just to witness the epic clash.

After his victory, Dara Singh arrived in Digboi as a personal guest of KB Kanuga. Standing tall and imposing, with a warm smile that belied his fearsome reputation in the ring, Dara Singh greeted the Digboi crowd with open arms.

"Mere apne from Digboi!" he boomed, referring to the people as his own. The club erupted in cheers, and it was a night to remember. The children, in particular, were in awe as Dara Singh regaled them with stories from his wrestling career.

Kanuga stood nearby, watching the scene unfold, feeling a deep sense of fulfilment. He was happy that through his initiatives, he had also woven a rich cultural fabric that connected the people to the wider world.

As the evening wound down, Dara Singh placed a hand on Kanuga's shoulder and said, "This place... it has heart, thanks to you."

Kanuga smiled, humbled by the compliment. "It's not just me. It's all of us, working together. That's what makes Digboi special."

Under his leadership, sportsmanship, community spirit, and a deep sense of togetherness flourished in Digboi. The town had become more than just a center for oil exploration—it was a thriving community, filled with opportunity, culture, and pride.

The real turning point came in 1953 when something monumental occurred - oil was discovered in Naharkatiya, about 40 kilometers west of Digboi. The discovery electrified Assam's oil community, offering the potential of vast oil reserves that could place the region on the global energy map.

One evening, as Kanuga was returning home from office, Anthony Gowan intercepted him at the gate, his eyes alight with excitement.

"KB, we've struck oil in Naharkatiya!" Gowan exclaimed.

Kanuga's heart raced. "Naharkatiya? That's incredible Tony!"

"It's more than incredible—it's a game-changer," Gowan said. "This could lead to a massive expansion of operations. The company has big plans, and this is just the beginning."

With the discovery of oil at Naharkatiya, the pace of operations quickened, but the excitement of the find was soon met with daunting logistical challenges. The oil wells lay on the south bank of the Burhi Dihing River, while the company's temporary base, Baruah Camp, remained on the north bank. Every day, workers journeyed from Digboi, crossing the unpredictable river by boat to reach the oil fields.

There was a railway bridge spanning the Burhi Dihing, but no road bridge yet. People could walk across it, but transporting machinery and vehicles required large boats and ferries. The river, calm on some days, became treacherous on others.

One morning, Kewalram, accompanied by a group of engineers, made the routine journey across the river in a small wooden boat. The water was unusually rough that day, and the wind lashed against their faces.

Ramesh, a young engineer sitting beside Kewalram, eyed the churning river nervously.

"Sir," Ramesh began, his voice wavering, "do you think we'll ever have a proper setup on the south bank? This boat ride feels like a gamble every time."

Kewalram smiled softly, his gaze fixed on the wide river ahead. "It is risky," he acknowledged, his voice steady. "But this is only a temporary situation. Once the infrastructure catches up with the oil we've discovered, things will be different."

Ramesh nodded, though doubt still flickered in his eyes. "A bridge would change everything, sir," he said hopefully.

Kewalram knew the young engineer wasn't wrong. A bridge was indeed being constructed by the government, but it was moving at a slow pace—far slower than they could afford. Stepping off the boat onto the muddy southern bank, Kewalram's thoughts churned as wildly as the river's current. The daily crossings were becoming more dangerous, and he could feel the toll it was taking on his team.

Later that evening, he called a meeting with his senior engineers. "We can't wait for the bridge," Kewalram said, his voice firm. "We need to act now."

Determined to solve the issue, Kewalram spearheaded the construction of residential quarters on the south bank, near the Naharkatiya wells. Within a few months, the workers and engineers no longer had to brave the hazardous river crossings everyday. The new quarters offered a sense of safety and stability, allowing the team to focus on the rapidly expanding operations without the ever-present threat of the unpredictable river.

One evening, Ramesh, now comfortably settled in his new quarters, stopped by Kewalram's office, "You were right, sir," he said, a grateful smile on his face. "This is exactly what we needed."

Kewalram, sipping tea on his veranda, looked up at the young man. "I told you, Ramesh," he replied with a smile, "it was only temporary."

After the independence, India's oil exploration future appeared uncertain. When Prime Minister Jawaharlal Nehru consulted global oil giants like MOBIL, EXXON, SHELL, and British Petroleum, their expert opinion was grim. They concluded that India did not have significant oil reserves, and that oil exploration and production were too complex and risky for a newly independent nation. They advised India to focus on importing crude oil from oil-rich countries while building refineries to meet its domestic requirements. Nehru believed their assessment, and as a result, oil exploration received little attention in the first two Five Year Plans.

However, this belief was challenged in 1953 when Assam Oil Company (A.O.C.) successfully drilled a deep well—around 10,000 feet—in the Naharkatiya area. It was the first successful oil well drilled in independent India with the potential for commercial production. News of this discovery reached K. D. Malviya, then the Union Minister of Chemical and Fertilizers, who immediately air-dashed to Dibrugarh to see the well for himself.

With no bridge over the Dihing River, Malviya crossed on a steamer boat and arrived to examine the well in Naharkatiya. To his utter surprise, the key figures responsible for this breakthrough were Indian experts—W. B. Maitre and A. B. Dasgupta—who had applied proper geoscientific methods rather than mere luck, as had been the case with Digboi's accidental discovery years earlier. Maitre and Dasgupta explained how they had used modern techniques to identify oil reserves in Naharkatiya, completely overturning the previously held belief that India's oil potential was insignificant.

Returning to Delhi, Malviya announced the discovery of oil outside Digboi and relayed his experience to Prime Minister Nehru, convincing him to prioritize oil exploration in future national plans. Fortuitously, around the same time, Russia expressed willingness to assist India in its oil exploration endeavors, paving the way for the establishment of the Oil and Natural Gas Commission (ONGC) in 1956 under full government control.

This shift in Government's approach marked the beginning of India's journey toward energy self-sufficiency, with Duliajan and Digboi at its heart.

By 1958, excitement in Assam's oil industry reached a new high. The discovery of oil in Moran, approximately 50 kilometers from Nahorkatiya, reverberated through the region. This second major find confirmed what many had long suspected—Assam was sitting on vast, untapped oil reserves. The region, once quiet, was now poised to become a cornerstone of India's burgeoning energy sector.

Amid this surge of activity, K.B. Kanuga's calm leadership became indispensable. His sharp intellect and deep understanding of both technical and operational aspects earned him the respect of colleagues and superiors alike. He was known for being measured, thoughtful, and able to navigate the complex intersections of fieldwork and business.

One afternoon, Gowan, his longtime mentor, called Kewalram into his office. Gowan's usual smile was absent, replaced by a more serious demeanor.

"KB, we need to talk," Gowan said, motioning for him to sit. There was a weight to his words, as if they carried the gravity of something momentous.

"With the discoveries at Nahorkatiya and now Moran, the Indian government is taking a keen interest in our operations. They're pushing for a joint venture," Gowan began.

Kanuga's brow furrowed. "A joint venture?"

"Yes," Gowan continued. "Between Burmah Oil and the Government of India. Two-thirds of the shares for Burmah, one-third for the government. The new company will be called Oil India Private

Limited. It's going to be a massive project, KB, and we need people who understand both the technical and the commercial sides of the business."

He paused, his gaze locking onto Kanuga's. "And I want you to be a part of this."

Kanuga leaned forward slightly, his curiosity piqued. "Tony, you think I can help with this?"

"I don't think, KB—I know," Gowan replied, his voice steady. "You've proven yourself time and again. We need you to help lead this transition." Kanuga absorbed the words. This was a turning point, not just for the company but for the country.

Kewalram Kanuga had already achieved a groundbreaking milestone in 1957-58 when he became the first Indian to serve as Acting General Manager of the Assam Oil Company (AOC). His leadership extended beyond routine operations; he played a pivotal role in shaping the oil industry in India. As an AOC employee, he was involved in high-stakes committees, including the Refinery Location Committee and negotiations that culminated in the formation of Oil India Limited. He contributed to the Promotion Agreement, asset valuation assessments, and the establishment of service terms for the newly formed company. Each committee offered him a unique platform to collaborate with government officials and industry experts, experiences he found deeply fulfilling.

On the 18th of February, 1959, Oil India Private Limited was officially born—a joint venture that marked a new chapter in India's oil industry. Kanuga, with his rare blend of field expertise and business acumen, was appointed to a pivotal leadership role as Manager, Oil Matters (MOM).

As Oil India Ltd. grew, so too did Kanuga's influence. He was at the forefront of a transformation that would shape the country's petroleum future. The incorporation of Oil India on that February day was more than a bureaucratic milestone—it signalled the dawn of a new era in India's energy landscape. The company, a partnership between the Government of India and The Burmah Oil Company, was registered in Shillong, with the primary task of extracting oil from the rich fields of Nahorkatiya, Hoogrijan, and Moran. This crude would fuel the public-sector refineries planned for Assam and Bihar.

It was no small feat. Already, fifty wells had been drilled by the Assam Oil Company, and their assets were now transferred to the newly formed Oil India Ltd. The journey leading up to this point had been one of intense negotiations and dedication, culminating in the signing of the crucial agreements on the 14th of January, 1958, followed by the supplemental agreement and formal registration on the 16th of February, 1959, in New Delhi. The signing ceremony, held with the gravitas such an occasion deserved, was attended by key figures, including W.P.G. Machlachlan, General Manager of the Assam Oil Company, and K.K. Sahni, Joint Secretary of the Ministry of Mines and Fuel.

With its headquarters established in Digboi, Oil India Ltd. was built on an authorized capital of 50 crores, divided into shares—two-thirds provided by The Burmah Oil Company, and the remaining third by the Government of India. But beyond these numbers lay a deeper purpose: to harness the vast energy resources beneath Assam's soil for the nation's progress.

Just five days after its official incorporation, on the 23rd of February 1959, the first Board Meeting of Oil India Private Ltd was convened in Digboi. W P G Machlachlan was elected Chairman of the Board of Directors, joined by G.N.S. Robertson, K.K. Sahni, Rana K.D.N. Singh, R.W. Watcher, and, of course, K.B. Kanuga. The air was thick with the promise of what was to come. Kanuga, ever the visionary, saw in this partnership the beginning of something far greater—a future where Assam's oilfields would fuel not only machines, but the dreams of a growing, independent India.

Despite the excitement, challenges remained. The headquarters was still in Digboi, with workers traveling daily through dense jungle to reach the oil fields. Kewalram knew this was unsustainable. The temporary setup at Baruah Camp near Tipling, built as a transit camp with a few bamboo and thatch houses had served its purpose for a time, could no longer keep up with the growing scale of operations.

One evening, as he sat with Ganga on their porch, Kewalram shared his thoughts.

"We need to build the headquarters closer to the oil fields," he said, staring out into the distance. "Baruah Camp was always meant to be temporary. We need something permanent, a settlement near Naharkatiya."

Ganga listened carefully, her trust in him unwavering. "And how will you make that happen?"

Kewalram smiled, determination glinting in his eyes. "We'll build something new. A town, a community where people can live and work close to the heart of the action."

"If anyone can do it, it's you Kanuga ji," Ganga said softly. Kewalram's heart filled with confidence hearing these words.

As 1958 came to a close, Kanuga's vision for a new headquarters near the oil fields began to take shape. The discovery of oil in Moran, coupled with the increasing scale of operations at Naharkatiya, solidified the need for a more permanent base of operations. It was clear that continuing to run the fields from Digboi was no longer feasible.

Kewalram Kanuga had been at the forefront of planning every step of the way, and as Oil India Limited moved into a new era, he remained the steady hand guiding its course. The future of Assam's oil industry had never looked brighter, and with Kewalram Kanuga leading the charge, that future was ready to take flight.

Chapter 5:
Building Duliajan (1958-1969)

The excitement around Oil India Limited was palpable. With the discovery of oil in Moran following Naharkatiya, Assam had become the centre of India's growing energy ambitions. But as Kewalram Kanuga knew well, discovering oil was only part of the challenge. The infrastructure to support these operations was sorely lacking, and the temporary setup at Baruah Camp, near Tipling with its daily travel through jungles from Digboi and then boat crossings across the Burhi Dihing River, was no longer sustainable.

One evening, as Kanuga sat in a meeting with the senior leadership of Oil India Limited, the topic of a new headquarters came to the forefront.

"We need a permanent solution," Mr. Machlachlan, the Chairman, said firmly. "Baruah Camp has served its purpose, but it's time to build a permanent settlement closer to the railway station."

Kanuga nodded in agreement. "We're wasting precious time and resources with the people travelling between Digboi and Duliajan every day. It's inefficient and dangerous for the workers. We need a base that allows us to work without interruption."

Machlachlan leaned back in his chair. "And where do you propose we build this new base?"

Kanuga paused, gathering his thoughts. "Sir, there's land near the Duliajan railway station. It's a place close to the operations at Naharkatiya and Moran, and the railway station will make transportation much easier. It's also not far away from Baruah Camp, so the transition will be smoother."

A murmur of agreement spread through the room.

Machlachlan's eyes lit up. "Duliajan... that could work. But where will we get the land?"

"Sir, we can procure it from Zaloni Tea Estate," Kanuga replied. "The estate has vast stretches of land, and it's ideally located for what we need."

The decision was made. Oil India Limited would build a new township near Duliajan railway station, close to the tea estates and the operations. It was a bold move, one that would take immense planning and effort, but it was necessary to keep pace with the growing demands of the oil fields.

Kewalram Kanuga found himself at the centre of this monumental task. His experience in both technical and managerial roles made him the perfect candidate to oversee the development of the new township. It wasn't just about creating office buildings or oil infrastructure—it was about building a community.

One evening, as Kewalram and Ganga sat together after dinner in their bungalow in Digboi, he shared the news.

"We're going to build a township in Duliajan," he said, his voice filled with excitement.

Ganga raised an eyebrow, intrigued. "A township? You mean, not just offices?"

"No, not just offices," Kewalram replied, smiling. "We're creating a place where people can live, work, and raise their families. There will be houses, schools, hospitals... even clubs and playgrounds. It'll be a community, a real home for the people working in the oil fields."

Ganga's eyes softened. "That sounds beautiful. You've always dreamed of building something like this, haven't you?"

Kewalram nodded. "Yes. And now we have the chance."

In the following months, the land acquisition from Zaloni Tea Estate began. The sprawling tea gardens, with their lush green slopes and winding paths, were soon marked for the construction of the new township. Kanuga oversaw the entire process, negotiating with the estate owners, planning the layout, and ensuring that the needs of the workers were prioritized.

It wasn't easy. Building a township from scratch came with its own set of challenges—logistical, financial, and political. But Kanuga was determined.

"We'll need proper housing for the workers," Kanuga said one day during a planning meeting. "These people are the backbone of our operations. They deserve to live comfortably, not just in makeshift quarters."

The engineers and architects nodded, taking notes.

"We'll also need a market, a school and a hospital," Kewalram continued. "We're not just building for the present. We're building for the future. The families that move here will need education and healthcare."

Machlachlan, sitting at the head of the table, smiled approvingly. "You're thinking long-term, KB. That's why we trust you with this."

By the end of 1960, construction on the new township was well underway. The land from Zaloni Tea Estate had been transformed into a carefully planned industrial town. Streets were being laid out, houses built, and key infrastructure was slowly taking shape. Kewalram made frequent visits to the site, overseeing every detail, from the layout of the main offices to the placement of homes and recreational areas.

One afternoon, as he walked through the construction site, he ran into Anthony Gowan, who was also overseeing the construction works for the office buildings.

"KB" Gowan called out, walking over to him, "this place is coming along faster than I expected. You've done an incredible job."

Kanuga smiled, wiping sweat from his brow. "Tony, we've still got a long way to go, but we're getting there. I want this place to be more than just functional. I want it to feel like home for the workers and their families."

Gowan nodded, looking around at the newly laid roads and the skeletons of buildings beginning to rise. "And that's exactly why you're the right man for the job."

As 1961 approached, the township of Duliajan was nearing completion. The houses were almost ready, and the new township and offices were being built. A market area called 'the OIL market' had been developed, a school was being planned, and a hospital to provide medical care for the community was on the horizon.

One evening, as Kanuga stood on an elevated platform overlooking the construction site, Mr. Dutta, a senior civil engineer working on the site, walked up to join him. The cool evening breeze ruffled Dutta's shirt as he stood beside Kanuga, surveying the town below.

"It's coming together nicely," Dutta said, his eyes scanning the layout of the nearly completed township.

Kanuga nodded, his heart swelling with pride. "It's more than I ever imagined. This will be the heart of Oil India's operations for years to come."

Dutta smiled, clearly impressed. "You've overseen something remarkable here, Kanuga Sir. A place where people can live, work, and grow their families."

Kanuga smiled in return, glancing at Dutta with appreciation. "It's not just me, Dutta. This is the result of the hard work of so many, including you. This is for all of us."

They stood together in quiet satisfaction, watching as the township that would soon become home to countless families took its final shape.

In the years that followed, Oil India Limited continued to evolve, reflecting both the growing importance of Assam's oil fields and India's strategic ambitions in the energy sector. The transformation became most evident on 27th July 1961, when the Government of India, through a second supplemental agreement, increased its share in Oil India to fifty percent, becoming an equal partner with Burmah Oil. This shift marked a major milestone in the company's history, and the name officially changed from Oil India Private Limited to Oil India Limited.

The new Board of Directors now included a blend of Indian and Burmah Oil representatives: Mr. M. J. Condon, Mr. G. N. S. Robertson, Mr. V. E. W. Stewart, Mr. N. N. Wanchoo, Mr. W. B. Maitre, Mr. K. B. Kanuga, Mr. A. C. Gowan, Mr. Rana K. D. N. Singh, and Mr. K. K. Sahni. The agreement, which had reshaped Oil India, also rendered several prior agreements inoperative, including the Promotion Agreement of 14th January 1958 and the Supplemental Agreement of 16th February 1959. Only Clause 12 of the second supplemental agreement remained active, ensuring the continuation of critical operations.

The Board of Directors, split right down the middle—eight directors, with equal representation from both The BOC and the Government of India. That kind of balance wasn't common in those days, but it worked beautifully. The BOC's managing director and Govt of India's finance director, each serving for five years, with the chairmanship alternating every year between the two partners—it was seamless. Mr. Khandubhai Desai, who became chairman in 1961, was a Member of Parliament, and he brought such a keen sense of diplomacy and leadership to the table.

Under the new terms, the agreement stipulated the supply of crude oil to proposed refineries at Gauhati and Barauni, targeting an annual output of 2.75 million tons, while the Digboi Refinery was to receive up to 435,000 tons per annum. The construction of the pipeline to transport the crude oil to these refineries was entrusted to Burmah Oil Co (Pipelines) Ltd, part of the Burmah Oil India Trading Group. According to the agreement signed on 29th October 1959, pipeline construction would be completed under Burmah Oil's management, with Oil India taking over once a one-year warranty period had passed after commissioning.

As Oil India grew, it began to sever its dependence on the older Assam Oil Company. On 9th March 1962, J. C. Finlay became the first Managing Director of Oil India Limited, symbolizing the company's new era of leadership. At the same time, a new chapter opened in the geographical heart of the business. Oil India cut its umbilical cord from Digboi and the Assam Oil Company by establishing its own offices and residential headquarters in a newly planned township at Duliajan. By the first half of the 1960s, the company had fully shifted to Duliajan, marking a significant step in becoming an independent entity, fully equipped to handle the expanding responsibilities of managing India's crucial oil assets.

The second supplemental agreement and the subsequent move to Duliajan were transformative for Oil India. Under the leadership of visionaries like K.B. Kanuga, the company not only grew in stature but also laid the foundation for India's future energy independence.

Chapter 6:
The Roots of Duliajan

As the new township of Duliajan neared completion, Kewalram Kanuga often found himself wondering about the history of the land that would soon host the bustling operations of Oil India Limited. For Kanuga, building a future meant more than just constructing roads and buildings—it meant understanding the roots of the place. He always felt that the region around Duliajan was steeped in stories of a past long before the oil industry arrived, and Kanuga was eager to know that history.

One evening, after a long day of overseeing operations, Kanuga decided to take a walk through the newly developed streets of Duliajan. The soft twilight bathed the surroundings in a warm glow, and he paused to appreciate the progress made. As he strolled, he noticed a familiar face – Manik Neog, one of the senior workmen from the region, carrying some tools back to the storage shed.

"Good Evening, Manik," Kanuga greeted him with a nod.

"Good evening, Sir," Manik replied with a smile, wiping the sweat from his brow.

They fell into step, walking together in comfortable silence for a while.

After a few minutes, Kanuga broke the silence. "Manik, you've lived here your whole life, haven't you?"

Manik nodded, "Yes, sir. Born and raised here, from long before the new township was built."

Kanuga's curiosity piqued. "Tell me something, Manik. Do you know where the name Duliajan comes from? I've heard stories, but I'd like to know from someone who knows the land."

Manik's face brightened. "Ah, Duliajan… yes, there's a story behind it. A long time ago, before the British or oil came here, this land was part of the Ahom Kingdom. The nobles used to pass through here, traveling along the Burhi Dihing."

Kanuga listened attentively as Manik continued.

"They didn't travel like we do now, Sir. Back then, the nobles were carried in palanquins by men called 'Dulias.' These Dulias were strong and skilled, carrying their masters across rivers and forests. When they reached this area, they would rest near a small rivulet. That place became known for the Dulias who would stop here with their noble masters. Over time, people began calling the small rivulet as 'Duliajan'— and this place got its name from the rivulet".

Kanuga's eyes widened in fascination. "So, the name comes from the people who carried the nobles, not the nobles themselves?"

Manik nodded. "Yes, sir. The Dulias were respected for their service, and that's how the name stuck. This land holds many stories from long ago."

Kanuga smiled, feeling a deeper connection to the place he was helping build. "It's amazing how history lives on in ways we never expect," he mused. "Here we are, creating something new, and yet, the past still shapes the land."

Manik grinned. "It's true, Sir. We may be building new roads and homes, but the stories of the past remain in the soil."

As they continued walking, Kanuga felt a sense of fulfilment. Not only was he part of a modern project, but he was also connected to the rich history of the region—a history he now understood a little better, thanks to Manik's tale.

Kanuga told this story to his engineers and workmen. As word of the story spread, curiosity about the land's history grew among the workers and engineers labouring to bring Duliajan to life. One afternoon, during a break, a small group gathered around Kanuga, eager to learn more about the land they were building on.

"Sahab," a young worker named Mohan asked, his voice full of wonder, "we've heard you talk about the Ahom nobles. Can you tell us more? How did they live here?"

Kanuga smiled at the eager faces surrounding him. "The Ahoms were a powerful kingdom, and this area was one of the many places they passed through. The Burhi Dihing River was vital to them—it wasn't just a waterway, but a trade route, a lifeline that connected people and goods. The nobles travelled in style, carried by the Dulias in their palanquins, stopping by the rivulet to rest. That's where the connection to this place comes from."

The workers listened intently, their eyes widening with a newfound appreciation for the land.

"So, we're continuing their journey, in a way?" Mohan asked, his grin spreading.

Kanuga smiled. "In a sense, yes. The nobles never imagined that one day, this place would become the center of India's oil industry. But here we are, building on their legacy. The river that brought them here centuries ago still flows, just as it did then, connecting the past and the present."

As Duliajan grew, so did the sense of belonging among its residents. The stories Kanuga shared began to weave themselves into the fabric of everyday life, turning the township from a mere workplace into a home—a place rooted in history, yet looking toward the future.

In the evenings, after the day's work was done, Kewalram Kanuga often found himself standing at the edge of the Burhi Dihing, watching the river flow lazily through the landscape. He would close his eyes and imagine the palanquins of the Ahom nobles, the Dulias trudging along the riverbanks, their voices carried by the wind. It was as though the river whispered the stories of those who had come before, reminding him that the land had always been a place of significance.

One evening, as he stood by the river, Ganga joined him. She touched his arm gently, noticing the distant look in his eyes.

"What are you thinking about?" she asked softly.

Kewalram smiled, turning to her. "About this place. How the Ahom nobles traveled these lands, and how we're continuing their legacy by building this township. It's incredible to think that the same river that brought them here is now witnessing the birth of something new."

Ganga gazed out at the river, her eyes reflecting its quiet flow. "It's amazing, isn't it? To be a part of something so much bigger than ourselves."

"That's exactly it," Kewalram said, his voice filled with warmth. "We're writing a new chapter in the history of this land. Duliajan isn't just a name on a map. It's alive, filled with stories—past and present."

As 1961 drew to a close, Duliajan was nearly complete. The township buzzed with life, and Oil India Limited began shifting its operations from the temporary camps at Baruah to the new headquarters. The township, once an idea sketched on paper, had become a reality—a symbol of progress deeply rooted in the land's rich history.

For Kewalram Kanuga, the completion of Duliajan was not just a professional achievement. It was a deeply personal one. He had not only overseen the building of a township but had also brought the stories of the past to life, ensuring that the people who now called Duliajan home understood its significance.

Duliajan was no longer just a place of work—it had become a living, breathing community, connected to centuries of history and the aspirations of the future. And as Kewalram stood by the Burhi Dihing, watching the river flow, he knew that he had helped build something that would last for generations to come.

Chapter 7:
Initial Years of building Duliajan – Through Ups and Downs

The 1960s ushered in a period of immense progress for both Kewalram Kanuga and his wife Ganga. While personal challenges tested their resilience, Kewalram's professional achievements with Oil India were nothing short of groundbreaking.

In 1961, Oil India was marking historic milestones, with Kewalram Kanuga leading several of its pivotal projects. One of his most notable accomplishments was the commissioning of India's first gas turbine-based power generating unit, a move that set the foundation for future innovations in the energy sector.

One evening, Kewalram sat with C. R. Jagannathan, or "Jag" as he was fondly called, a geologist and the head of the Geological Department. As they shared tea, they reflected on the remarkable progress since their arrival in Duliajan.

"We've come a long way, Jag," Kanuga said, his voice filled with pride as he glanced at the bustling oil township. "From building this place out of the tea gardens to commissioning the world's first crude oil conditioning plant here."

Jagannathan nodded with a smile. "And the pipeline from Naharkatiya to Barauni—720 miles! That's a colossal achievement, KB."

"The first section, 250 miles from Naharkatiya to Noonmati, is already operational. Soon the entire pipeline will connect Assam's oil fields to the heart of India," Kanuga said with excitement. "This project will transform not just Assam, but the entire country."

Jagannathan leaned back, thoughtfully. "The challenges we faced building that pipeline—people will find them hard to imagine."

Kanuga smiled. "No bridges, no proper roads. We had to transport everything by water to Pandu, and then load it onto trains and trucks to reach its destination."

"And the rivers," Jagannathan remarked, "Nearly 78 major ones, starting with the Burhi Dihing and even the Brahmaputra."

Kanuga nodded. "Yes, and the Teesta, Torsa, Mahananda, and Kosi further down. We had to improvise."

Jagannathan grinned. "I heard they even replaced jeep tyres with railway wheels to cross the rivers by railway bridges."

Kanuga laughed. "Crazy people, but this innovative idea worked. Soon, oil will flow across those rivers, connecting Assam's oilfields with the rest of the nation."

The two men sat in silence for a moment, absorbing the magnitude of what they were accomplishing. Finally, Kanuga spoke. "And now, the refinery at Noonmati—it's almost ready."

Jagannathan raised an eyebrow. "It is India's first public sector refinery, Right?"

Kanuga nodded. "Yes, with Romanian assistance. It will process 0.75 million metric tonnes of crude per year, and they're planning to expand to 1.0 MMTPA. Prime Minister Nehru himself is coming to inaugurate it on January 1st, 1962. This refinery will produce everything from LPG to high-speed diesel. It's a game-changer."

"Wow, I Did not know that Nehru will be there." Jagannathan was excited.

"Yes," Kewalram confirmed. "Along with K. D. Malaviya, the Union Minister, and Romania's Minister Mr. Florescu. This is more than just oil—it's about building a self-sustaining industry."

As they continued to reflect, Jagannathan said quietly, "From the discoveries at Naharkatiya and Moran to this... it's incredible how far we've come, KB."

Kanuga's eyes gleamed. "Yes. Noonmati refinery in Gauhati symbolizes the future. What we've started in the fields, this refinery will carry forward for the entire nation."

The conversation ended in silence, both men fully aware of the historic weight of their work. As the sun set over Duliajan, they knew that a new dawn was rising—not just for Assam, but for India's energy independence.

On January 1, 1962, Prime Minister Nehru inaugurated the Gauhati Refinery.

The same day, that is 1st January, 1962, Oil India Ltd. officially shifted its headquarters to Duliajan from Digboi. Kewalram Kanuga was promoted to be the first General Manager of Oil India Ltd, marking the beginning of a new era for both the company and the oil-rich region of Assam.

However, Kanuga's journey to this position was not without its setbacks. Despite being officially designated General Manager on January 1, 1962, bureaucratic entanglements and political considerations delayed his formal recognition.

Even after assuming the role, Kanuga found himself in the midst of upheaval. The newly formed Board of Directors, split evenly between the Government of India and the Burmah Oil Company (B.O.C.), faced significant challenges. Labour strikes erupted after wage cuts, decisions driven by government-appointed directors. The strikes escalated into violence, culminating in a tragic clash that left a police constable dead. Amidst the turmoil, Kanuga became the target of baseless accusations, with some even alleging his complicity in the unrest. Resolute in his integrity, he confronted the accusations head-on, offering his resignation to R.P. Smith and demanding the freedom to clear his name. Smith, after consulting with senior officials, reaffirmed Kanuga's position, dismissing the allegations as unfounded.

Kanuga's early days as General Manager were anything but smooth. Political interference was rampant. Every politician, from ministers to local MLAs, seemed to have a vested interest in Oil India's operations. Requests for favors, jobs, and contracts poured in, often accompanied by veiled threats of complaints and investigations. Despite this, Kanuga remained steadfast, deftly navigating the complex web of expectations and demands.

Over time, Kanuga's resilience and vision began to bear fruit. The oil fields thrived under his leadership, and the organization gained a reputation for its efficiency and innovation. Looking back, those turbulent years became emblematic of his journey—proof of his ability to rise above the chaos and lay the foundation for Oil India's legacy.

But despite the success, new challenges emerged on the horizon. By 1962, geopolitical tensions were mounting in the region, and India faced threats from its northern neighbour, China. The Chinese military had advanced to Bomdila and was in striking distance from Tezpur, a town 300 Km away from Digboi. While there had been no direct attack on Assam's oil fields, the fear lingered.

One evening, as Kanuga sat in his office reviewing plans for the expansion of Oil India's operations, he received an urgent call. It was from the Assam state authorities.

"Mr. Kanuga," the voice on the other end said, heavy with concern. "We've received intelligence that the Chinese may target critical infrastructure in the northeast, including the Digboi refinery."

Kanuga's heart skipped a beat. "The Digboi refinery? How real is this threat?"

"We're not certain, but the refinery is one of the key facilities in the region. It would be a prime target if tensions escalate. We're advising heightened security and precautions."

Kanuga put down the phone, his mind racing. The refinery was crucial not just to Oil India but to the entire country's energy needs. If anything were to happen to it, the consequences would be devastating.

The next morning, Kanuga convened an emergency meeting with Mr. Anthony Gowan, CEO of Assam Oil Company, and the senior leadership at Oil India. The atmosphere in the room was tense.

"We can't take any chances," Gowan said, his voice firm. "The refinery must be protected at all costs."

Kanuga nodded in agreement. "We need to implement safety measures immediately. Evacuate non-essential personnel from the refinery and reinforce security. We should also set up a plan to safeguard the workers and their families in case of an attack."

The room fell silent for a moment as the gravity of the situation sank in. Oil had always been the lifeblood of India's economy, but now it had become a target in a growing geopolitical conflict.

"We'll coordinate with the local authorities and the military," Kanuga added. "But we need to reassure the people in Duliajan and Digboi that we're prepared for any eventuality. Panic won't help anyone."

As Chinese were advancing, in his address to the nation on All India Radio on November 20, 1962, Prime Minister Nehru said, "Huge Chinese armies have been marching in the northern part of NEFA. We have had reverses at Walong, Se La and today Bomdila, a small town in NEFA, has also fallen. We shall not rest till the invader goes out of India or is pushed out. I want to make that clear to all of you, and, especially our countrymen in Assam, to whom our heart goes out at this moment.

The news of Bomdila's fall spread like wildfire, reaching every household, every market, every gathering in Assam. The quiet town of Digboi, just 300 kilometers from Bomdila, was particularly shaken. Rumors swirled with increasing intensity, each one painting a dire picture of the Chinese advancing towards Assam and NEFA. The people of Duliajan and Naharkatiya, home to crucial oil fields, grew anxious, wondering if their quiet towns would soon find themselves on the frontline.

It became clear that even Duliajan and Naharkatiya oil fields, located relatively close to the conflict zone, could become the first target. The company's leadership made the difficult decision: families of the officers would be relocated for their safety. The goal was simple yet critical—to allow the officers to focus solely on their duties without the worry of their families' well-being hanging over their heads.

For Ganga and the children, this meant leaving their home and the life they knew behind. The Kanuga household had been a source of warmth, filled with laughter and love, but now it was time to face the unknown. Kewalram, though stoic as always, was torn between his duty and the safety of his family.

"Do you think, it is a good decision to leave this place?" Kewalram asked one evening, his voice low as he stood with Ganga on the veranda. The two gazed at the twilight sky, the tension between them palpable.

Ganga, ever the practical one, nodded. "It's for the best. We need to be safe, and you—you need to focus on your work. I'll take care of the children."

The decision was made swiftly. Ganga, along with their children, would board a small Dakota aircraft from Mohanbari airport in Dibrugarh, bound for Calcutta, where they would wait out the uncertain days ahead. The plane, a relic of the Second World War, was hastily repurposed for the evacuation. The seats were removed to accommodate more passengers, and each person was allowed just a single bag—one bag to hold the essentials of their life, while leaving behind everything else they knew.

As Ganga prepared to leave, the weight of the moment struck her. "One bag," she thought. How could she possibly fit their life into one bag?

She gathered only the most necessary items—some clothes, important documents, and a few personal belongings for the children.

The day of departure arrived, and the family made their way to the airstrip at Mohanbari. The sight of the small Dakota, waiting amidst the humid air, seemed surreal. Kewalram stood at a distance, his face lined with worry, but he hid it well. Ganga, with the children clinging to her, looked back at him one last time before boarding.

"I'll see you soon," she called out, trying to keep her voice steady.

Kewalram waved but said nothing. The weight of responsibility bore down on him, for he knew what lay ahead. Oil India's officers had been tasked with an unthinkable job—if the Chinese troops advanced into Assam, they were to "kill the wells" and destroy the properties. The instructions were clear: in the event of a takeover, the Chinese would not inherit the valuable oil-producing assets that could fuel their advance. It was a desperate plan, but it was the only way to prevent the resources from falling into enemy hands.

As the plane took off from the small airstrip, Kewalram stood rooted to the spot, watching the Dakota disappear into the horizon. He could only hope that the war would not reach their doorstep.

As tensions escalated, a new order from the top came down—a contingency plan for the worst-case scenario. If the Chinese forces came too close, there were instructions to kill all the producing wells and destroy the newly installed gas turbine-based power plant on short notice. It was the Scorched Earth Policy of the military which stipulated the destruction of anything thet may help the enemy. It was a drastic measure, aimed at ensuring that the Chinese couldn't gain control of these crucial assets. The evacuation notice was also served, and many people from other states who had come to work in the area began to leave.

Over the next few weeks, Kanuga and his team worked tirelessly to put safety protocols in place. Security was increased around the refinery, and evacuation drills were conducted to ensure that workers and their families knew what to do in an emergency. The people of Duliajan, though anxious, trusted Kanuga's leadership. He had guided them through the challenging transition from Digboi, and they believed he would keep them safe.

As the Chinese aggression loomed larger, the officers of Oil India worked day and night, mentally preparing for the worst-case scenario. The plan to kill the wells, to destroy the very assets they had spent their careers building and maintaining, weighed heavily on all of them. It wasn't just a professional task—it was personal. For these officers, the wells were not just numbers on a report or marks on a map. They were the lifeblood of the company, and many of the men had dedicated their entire working lives to their maintenance and success.

The mood in Duliajan became increasingly somber. While the people were quietly evacuated, the officers remained behind, determined to see their mission through. The weight of the task settled heavily on their shoulders. Conversations, once filled with optimism about new discoveries or technological advancements, turned dark and reflective.

Some of the officers struggled deeply with the idea of destroying their own work. For many, it felt like they were being asked to destroy a part of themselves. One evening, after another intense meeting to finalize the details of the destruction, Kewalram noticed a younger colleague, Ajit Kumar Sharma from the Electrical Department, sitting alone on the steps of the Oil India office, his face buried in his hands.

Kewalram approached him, quietly sitting down beside his colleague. The silence between them stretched on, punctuated only by the faint hum of the generator in the distance. Finally, Sharma spoke, his voice thick with emotion.

"I can't do it, Kanuga Sir. I just can't." His eyes were red, tears threatening to spill over. "We built this gas turbine-based power station... we put everything into making this work. And now, they want us to tear it all down. It's like they're asking us to destroy our own soul."

Kewalram placed a steady hand on Sharma's shoulder. He understood. The wells, the infrastructure, everything they had worked for, wasn't just a job—it was their legacy. And yet, they had no choice. The orders were clear: if the Chinese army advanced, the power station would be obliterated to prevent them from falling into enemy hands.

Sharma wasn't the only one who felt the strain. Across the camp, other officers were grappling with the same feelings. Some of them cried, unable to hold back the emotion of it all. These were men who had spent years, sometimes decades, designing, constructing, and perfecting the very facilities they were now tasked with destroying.

Kewalram stood up, offering Sharma a hand to help him up as well. "I know, Ajit. It's not fair, and it's not easy. But we have to remember why we're doing this. It's not for us. It's for the country. If this war continues, we can't let this oil fall into their hands."

Sharma looked up at him, his face etched with pain. "But what if it doesn't come to that? What if… all of this is for nothing?"

Kewalram nodded, understanding the depth of his colleague's sorrow. "Maybe it will be. But if the worst does happen, we need to be ready. We owe it to everyone—to our families, to the country—to make sure we do everything we can."

The night wore on, and the grim preparations continued. Maps were studied, wires were set, and the officers went about their work with heavy hearts. It was a task none of them ever wanted to do, but the weight of their responsibility kept them moving forward.

The officers, including Kewalram, knew the risk they were taking, but none of them were prepared for the emotional toll it would take. When the ceasefire was announced, and the Chinese forces stopped their advance, the collective sigh of relief was palpable. They would not have to destroy their wells after all. The oil fields of Digboi and

Duliajan were safe. But the emotional scars remained, a reminder of how close they had come to losing everything.

In Calcutta, Ganga and the children anxiously awaited news. The war had ended before it could touch their lives directly, but the emotional toll lingered. When Kewalram finally arrived to bring his family back to Duliajan, they embraced with a mix of relief and exhaustion.

"You did it Kanuga ji," Ganga said, resting her head on his shoulder. "You kept people of Dulaijan safe."

Kewalram, though proud of the work they had done to protect India's oil assets, could only nod. The war had left its mark on all of them, a reminder of how fragile their world could be. But through it all, the strength of family, the support of loved ones, and the unwavering sense of duty had guided them through the most uncertain of times.

One afternoon, as Kanuga and Gowan walked through the Digboi refinery, which continued to operate at full capacity, Gowan turned to him.

"You handled that situation remarkably well, KB," he said. "There was potential for panic, but you kept everything under control."

Kanuga smiled, though the stress of the past few months still lingered in his eyes. "It wasn't easy Tony. But we couldn't afford to lose focus. This refinery, the fields in Nahorkatiya and Moran—they're vital to the country."

Gowan nodded, clapping him on the back. "You've done more than anyone could have asked for."

Resistance and Relocation (1961–1962)

KB Kanuga's vision had finally materialized. The township, with its tree-lined avenues, well-planned residential quarters, schools, and hospitals, had transformed into a vibrant community, far removed from the provisional structures of Baruah Camp. As operations expanded in Naharkatiya and Moran, Oil India Limited firmly established itself as a major force in India's oil industry. The township of Duliajan emerged as a beacon of progress—a place poised to shape the future of India's energy sector.

Though the township of Duliajan was beautifully designed and brimming with potential, it was not immediately welcomed by everyone. For generations, the workers and their families had established comfortable lives in Digboi, a well-rooted town with schools, markets, and social networks. The prospect of uprooting and relocating to an unfamiliar township filled many with reluctance and uncertainty.

Kanuga had anticipated some resistance, but he was taken aback by how deep it ran. One morning, as he walked through the office corridors, he caught fragments of a conversation among the workers.

"I heard Duliajan is still under construction," one man grumbled. "Why should we leave Digboi? Everything we need is already here."

Another worker added, "My kids are in school here, and my wife has friends. Why uproot ourselves to move to some place out in the middle of nowhere?"

A third voice, softer but edged with fear, broke in. "Do you think Digboi is really safe? I heard rumors the Chinese might attack the refinery. What if we end up in a war zone?"

Kanuga sighed quietly. Their concerns were understandable. Digboi had been home to generations of oil workers, and the idea of leaving it all behind was hard enough. But now, with the threat of a Chinese attack, the stakes were even higher.

Later that day, Kanuga sat across from Anthony Gowan in his office. Gowan paced by the window, his expression tense with worry.

"KB," Gowan began, "the resistance is stronger than we expected. They don't want to leave Digboi."

Kanuga nodded, understanding the weight of the situation. "They've built their lives here, Tony. It's not just about comfort; it's about fear, too."

"Fear?" Gowan raised an eyebrow.

"The war," Kanuga replied. "They worry Digboi might be attacked. For some, moving to Duliajan feels safer, but they need more reassurance."

Gowan sighed, rubbing his temples. "We can't delay any longer. Operations in Naharkatiya and Moran are expanding rapidly, and we need the headquarters in Duliajan. How do we convince them?"

Kanuga thought for a moment. "We need to show them what Duliajan has to offer. They're afraid of the unknown. If we can demonstrate that Duliajan is more than a workplace—a real community with schools, markets, and a sense of security—they might feel more at ease."

Gowan tilted his head thoughtfully. "You think a tour might do the trick?"

"It's worth a try," Kanuga replied with confidently. "We can't just order them to move. We need to earn their trust."

The following week, tours were organized for the workers and their families. Several buses lined up, ready to take them to see the new township. On the first day, Kanuga stood by the buses, greeting the hesitant families as they boarded.

A woman approached, holding her young son's hand, her face filled with uncertainty. "Sahab, is it true there's a school in Duliajan?"

Kanuga smiled warmly. "Yes. The school is nearly finished and will be one of the best in the region. Your children will receive an excellent education there."

The woman nodded slightly, though traces of uncertainty lingered in her eyes.

As the buses pulled away from Digboi, murmurs spread among the passengers. One man leaned over to his wife and whispered, "It looks good, but will it really be like this when we move? I heard there's no hospital yet. They're still taking women to Digboi for childbirth. How can we rely on their promises?"

Hearing this, Kanuga turned to the couple and spoke gently. "I understand your concerns," he said. "But I assure you, this isn't just for show. Duliajan is being built to enhance your lives. You'll be closer to work, and once the township is fully functional, you'll have everything you need right there."

The man gave a reluctant nod, though the tension in his expression remained.

Over the following weeks, the tours and discussions began to soften the initial resistance. Gradually, the workers started to glimpse the potential Duliajan offered. But Kanuga knew that the real challenge would arise once the relocation process officially began.

One afternoon, as Kanuga and Gowan reviewed logistics together, Gowan leaned back in his chair with a sigh. "I didn't realize moving so many people would be this challenging. But we're making progress, thanks to your efforts, KB."

Kanuga smiled faintly. "It's not easy, but I believe once the first group settles in, the rest will follow."

Gowan nodded, though his expression remained serious. "We need everyone settled soon. Operations at Naharkatiya and Moran are growing faster than expected."

The day of the move finally arrived, with Kanuga and Gowan leading the effort, overseeing every detail. Special arrangements were arranged for families with young children and the elderly. Relocating over two thousand people was no small task, but thanks to meticulous planning, the transition got off to a smooth start.

There were still moments of doubt. One evening, as Kanuga walked through Digboi's residential quarters, a group of workers approached him.

"Sahab," one of them began hesitantly, "what if Duliajan doesn't work out? What if the promises aren't kept?"

Kanuga met each man's gaze, his voice calm and empathetic. "I understand your concerns, but I promise you, Duliajan is not just a workplace; it's a home. A place where your children will grow up with better schools, healthcare, and a strong community. We are building something lasting."

A man who had been silent until then spoke up. "You've never let us down before, Sahab. I'll trust you on this."

By the end of 1962, the relocation was complete. A total of 2,174 people had moved from Digboi to Duliajan. The once-quiet streets of the new township were now alive with activity. Children played in open fields, families shopped at the new market, and workers walked to their jobs without the strain of long commutes.

The collaboration between Gowan and Kanuga ensured a smooth and effective transition. Gowan later received recognition from the British government, awarded an Order of the British Empire (OBE) for his efforts, while Kanuga quietly continued his work, expecting no accolades. For him, the safety and well-being of his colleagues and their families was the only reward needed.

Despite the lack of recognition, the fulfillment Kanuga felt was undeniable. Oil India was growing, lives were protected, and a new chapter of prosperity was beginning in Duliajan and beyond. The 1960s marked a turning point, both for the company and for Kanuga, who continued to build, innovate, and serve without seeking the spotlight.

For Kanuga, the successful relocation was more than a logistical accomplishment—it was a testament to trust and perseverance. He had helped build more than a township; he had guided a community through one of the biggest transitions of their lives.

One evening, as he stood on the edge of the bustling township, looking out toward the distant river, Ganga joined him, as she often did.

"They're settling in," she said softly, watching a group of children play nearby.

Kewalram nodded, a deep sense of satisfaction filling him. "Yes, they are. It wasn't easy, but we did it."

Ganga smiled, leaning into him. "You've built more than just a township, Kanuga ji. You've built a home."

Chapter 8:
Heart of Duliajan

By early 1963, Duliajan was transforming from a mere construction site into a vibrant township. Neat rows of houses, bustling markets, and expanding public spaces began shaping the town, while residents who were initially hesitant now found themselves settling in, embracing their new lives.

One morning, as Kewalram Kanuga strolled through the newly opened OIL market, he overheard a conversation between two shopkeepers.

"Business is picking up," one of them said, adjusting his display of vegetables. "Ever since the families moved in, this place feels alive."

The other shopkeeper nodded with a smile. "I was worried at first, but Duliajan is turning into something special. My kids love the new school, and it's a relief having the hospital close by." Another shopkeeper chimed in, "I've opened a small bookstall, and it's doing quite well."

Kanuga smiled, heartened by these remarks. The town was taking root, yet he knew there was still more to accomplish.

That evening, he sat on the porch with his wife, Ganga, gazing out over the growing town. She sensed his thoughts. "You've done so much," she said softly, "but I can see you're thinking about what's next."

He sighed. "We've built houses and roads, but a true community needs more than that . It needs a spirit, something that gives people a sense of belonging and pride."

Ganga nodded thoughtfully. "And how do you plan to bring that to life?"

"Through arts, sports, and education," he replied. "We've built the physical foundation. Now, we need to create the heart of Duliajan."

In 1961, Zaloni Primary School was established, and by 1963, Oil India Higher Secondary School had opened, becoming a cornerstone of the community. Kanuga often visited, meeting teachers and overseeing progress. One afternoon, while walking through the schoolyard, he was greeted by the headmaster, Mr. Hare Krishna Das.

"Kanuga Sir," Das greeted warmly, shaking his hand, "we're truly honoured to have you with us. The school is thriving, all thanks to your support."

Kanuga smiled, his gaze on the children playing nearby. "This school is for them," he said. "They are the future of this township."

Das nodded. "We have some excellent teachers, and the students are eager to learn."

"Education is the foundation of everything," Kanuga replied. "If we get this right, everything else will follow."

As the school flourished, so did the cultural life of Duliajan. Driven by his passion for the arts, Kanuga invited some of Assam's most respected figures, including Dr. Bhupen Hazarika, to perform and enrich the community. One evening, at a Bihutoli gathering, the sounds of traditional Assamese music and songs filled the air. Residents who had once been strangers now sat together, drawn close by the rhythm of their shared heritage.

"This is what you meant, isn't it?" Ganga whispered to him.

Kanuga smiled softly. "Exactly. Music, sports, festivals—they connect people together. They turn a town into a home."

In 1964, Kanuga organized Duliajan's first public Bihu celebration. The beat of dhols and the call of pepa filled the air, and temporary pandals transformed a simple field into a vibrant festival ground. Officers and workers danced together, children played, and laughter rang through the night.

"I never thought I'd be dancing Bihu here," one worker remarked to his friend with a smile. "Feels like home now, doesn't it?"

His friend grinned. "Kanuga Saheb has given us more than just jobs. He's given us a life."

Dr. Bhupen Hazarika and Bishnu Prasad Rabha, two of Assam's most respected cultural icons, were invited as special guests, adding an unforgettable charm to the celebration. The success of this first Bihu gathering turned it into an annual tradition. That field became known as Bihutoli, a cultural landmark where the community gathered every spring to celebrate.

Kanuga's other passion was sports. Together with senior officials, he helped develop tennis courts, football fields, and even a nine-hole golf course. In 1964, at Kanuga's urging, the 'Oil India Football Eleven' team was formed, bringing the community closer through the joy of sports.

One of the most anticipated traditions was the Duliajan to Digboi cycle race, an event that strengthened the bonds within the community. As the first race was about to begin, Gowan, the CEO of AOC, clapped Kanuga on the back. "You've really started something here, KB. Look at them—all eager and excited."

Kanuga nodded, watching the cyclists line up. "That's the goal. We're not just building an oil company; we're building a community."

The whistle blew, and the cyclists set off, cheered on by crowds lining the streets. For Kanuga, it was yet another sign that Duliajan was becoming the place he had dreamed of—a place of connection, belonging, and pride.

By 1964, Duliajan had transformed into a vibrant township. What had once been met with hesitation by those relocating from Digboi had now become the heart of Oil India's operations. The community thrived, united by shared traditions and celebrations, a testament to the vision and leadership of Kewalram Kanuga.

Chapter 9:
The Prime Minister's Visit

On June 9, 1963, fate took an unexpected turn for Duliajan's story. Prime Minister Jawaharlal Nehru, who was on his way to the North East Frontier Agency (NEFA) present-day Arunachal Pradesh), found his journey interrupted by sudden, unpredictable weather.

This was a day that nearly didn't happen. Kewalram Kanuga had long dreamed of showcasing the oilfields at Duliajan to Prime Minister Nehru, hoping to display India's promising ambitions in oil exploration. Yet, with the Prime Minister's schedule packed tightly, Duliajan was not on his itinerary. The opportunity seemed destined to slip by. But Kanuga was determined; he wasn't one to let such a moment pass without a determined effort.

Nehru found himself grounded at Tezpur airport, accompanied by Assam's Chief Minister Bimala Prasad Chaliha and State Governor Vishnu Sahay, as they waited for the weather to clear for his scheduled flight to the forward areas. After that, he was set to visit Dibrugarh, where all preparations had been meticulously arranged.

Kewalram Kanuga, a man who never let an opportunity pass, saw this as a golden moment. "We must show Nehru what we're building here," he told his team, his eyes lighting up with excitement. "He's so close—right here. If we can bring him to Duliajan, we can show him the future we're shaping."

Kanuga promptly reached out to the Deputy Commissioner of Dibrugarh, asking if there was any way to bring Nehru to Duliajan before his scheduled visit to Dibrugarh town. The Deputy Commissioner was initially unsure, but agreed to make provisional security arrangements, just in case.

When Nehru's plane landed at Mohanbari, the Deputy Commissioner escorted Kanuga to meet Assam's Chief Minister, B. P. Chaliha, who was traveling with Nehru. Sensing his moment, Kanuga made his case. "Sir, I'd like to invite the Prime Minister to visit the oilfields at Duliajan. He's visited Dibrugarh many times but has yet to see our new operations," he said sincerely.

The Chief Minister smiled, replying, "Come with me. I'll introduce you to Panditji. If you can persuade him, I have no objections." With a swift check on the security arrangements, everything was set in motion.

As Kanuga finally stood before the Prime Minister, he felt the weight of the moment. This was his one chance. "Sir," he began with determination, "you've visited Dibrugarh many times. Why not see the new oilfields at Duliajan, where the Government of India shares a 50% stake with the Burmah Oil Company?"

Nehru hesitated—Duliajan wasn't part of his schedule, and time was short. But before Kanuga could feel the pang of disappointment, Nehru exchanged a glance with Chief Minister Chaliha. With a thoughtful nod, he said, "Alright, I'll go. But first, I'd like to meet the children."

Kanuga's heart soared. Soon, the IAF helicopters were prepped, their blades whirring in anticipation of the unplanned journey to Duliajan. Kanuga found himself sharing one helicopter with the Prime Minister, Governor Vishnu Sahay, and Chief Minister Chaliha. The rest of the party, including press members from Delhi, followed in the other helicopters.

News of Nehru's visit spread through Duliajan like wildfire, filling the township with excitement. Workers lined the streets, and students from the newly founded Oil Higher Secondary School eagerly prepared to welcome the Prime Minister. For the people of Duliajan, this was more than just a prestigious visit—it was a recognition of their hard work and dedication to the country's progress.

When Nehru's helicopter finally landed on the football field, later renamed Nehru Maidan in his honor, the atmosphere was electric. As the helicopter door opened, the Prime Minister stepped out, accompanied by Chief Minister Chaliha and Governor Vishnu Sahay, to a heartfelt welcome from senior officials of Oil India Ltd., including C.R. Jagannathan, Ajit Kumar Sharma, and others.

Upon landing, Nehru's gaze was immediately drawn to a group of children from the Oil Higher Secondary School, eagerly gathered to give him a guard of honor. Known for his affection for children, Nehru walked toward them with a broad, welcoming smile. A young girl, eyes wide with awe, shyly stepped forward, holding a bouquet tightly in her hands.

Nehru knelt down to her level and asked gently, "What is your name?"

"Kalpana," she whispered, her voice barely above a murmur.

With a warm smile, Nehru placed a kind hand on her head. "Study hard, Kalpana," he encouraged. "You and your friends are the future of this country."

The children beamed with pride, their young hearts swelling at the moment. That brief but heartfelt interaction left an indelible mark on them—a memory to cherish for the rest of their lives. They had experienced a once-in-a-lifetime encounter with the Prime Minister himself.

The day had been flawless so far. Kewalram Kanuga felt a swell of pride as he stood beside Prime Minister Nehru, guiding him through the operations at Duliajan's oilfields. This was the moment he had envisioned for years—a chance to show the nation's leader that Indian expertise could handle the complexities of oil exploration and production.

With his characteristic curiosity, Nehru expressed a desire to see the operations up close. The group made their way to one of the oil collecting stations, led by Mr. Leslie Bond, the Production Superintendent.

As they stood before the intricate machinery, Mr. Bond carefully explained each step of the process. The group listened attentively as he pointed to the final vessel, where the crude oil would flow to storage tanks.

Suddenly, Nehru's eyes lit up with interest, and he turned to Mr. Bond. "Can you open the nozzle?" he asked. "I'd like to see the oil actually flow out."

A brief pause followed as the group exchanged cautious glances. Though simple, Nehru's request carried a bit of risk. What if something went wrong? Any minor issue could stop the flow—an embarrassing scenario in front of the Prime Minister.

Mr. Bond hesitated briefly, but with an encouraging nod from Kanuga, he stepped forward. Taking a steady breath, he opened the nozzle with care, and everyone held their breath.

To their immense relief, oil flowed smoothly into the bottle. Smiles spread through the group, and Nehru, sensing the earlier tension, let out a soft chuckle. "Ah, there it is. You've done well."

The group collectively exhaled, the weight of the moment lifting, and pride filled the air.

Kewalram shared a meaningful glance with Mr. C. R. Jagannathan, who had been quietly watching the interaction unfold. Jagannathan's eyes shone with pride for Kanuga's accomplishments and the tireless efforts that had helped bring Duliajan's oilfields to life.

The Prime Minister was then shown a detailed presentation on the complex oil field development across Oil India's Mining Lease Area, covering about 500 square miles in Naharkatiya, Moran, and Hoogrijan. The briefing also included exploration activities spanning

1,200 square miles in Doomdooma and proposed explorations in the NEFA region.

Nehru also toured Duliajan's industrial and residential areas, including a visit to the gas turbine power station– the first of its kind in India and the crude oil pump station, part of the 720-mile-long crude oil pipeline system.

After touring the oil fields, Nehru's curiosity was drawn to the plans for the new township—a project close to Kanuga's heart. With a mix of anticipation and pride, Kanuga approached Nehru and unrolled the blueprint. "Sir, these are our plans for Duliajan," he began. "We're creating a self-sustaining community where employees and their families can live, work, and grow while contributing to the nation's progress."

Nehru examined the layout thoughtfully, nodding in approval. "A township for the people," he said softly. "This is the kind of vision that shapes futures."

Kanuga's heart swelled with pride as the Prime Minister turned to him with a smile. "You've built something truly remarkable here, Kanuga ji," Nehru remarked. "This is where work and life can harmonize."

After the tour, Nehru, Chaliha, and Sahay were welcomed for lunch at Kanuga's bungalow, a setting that exuded the warmth and simplicity of Duliajan. Senior officials of Oil India and their spouses joined, adding to the sense of camaraderie. As they dined, Nehru noticed Kanuga's older children, Giridharilal, Leela, Lakshman and A B Dasgupta's son Udayan watching the gathering with awe from the sidelines.

"Kanuga ji," Nehru said thoughtfully, "you've built more than just oil fields here. You've built a future for these families."

After a warm and heartfelt meal, Nehru rose to leave, but not before offering Kanuga his full support. "You have my backing for this township, Kanuga ji. Let's make this vision a reality."

As the day came to a close, the Prime Minister and his party boarded helicopters bound for Dibrugarh, where Nehru was scheduled to spend the night at the Circuit House.

Later that evening, Kanuga joined Nehru at a dinner hosted by the Assam Government. The atmosphere was lively, with the soft clinking of glasses and murmured conversations. At one point, Nehru took Kanuga aside, a warm smile crossing his face.

"I'm glad you brought me to Duliajan," he said softly, his tone reflective. "It gave me the chance to see your work firsthand. You're doing commendable work."

Kewalram felt an immense sense of accomplishment. The Prime Minister's words had meant everything—it wasn't just about showcasing the oilfields but proving that Indian skill and determination could meet the formidable challenges of oil exploration.

As the night grew still, Kewalram reflected on the day. What made it truly special wasn't just Nehru's visit; it was the validation of years of hard work and the fulfillment of a dream to bring recognition to the people of Duliajan and their efforts. In Nehru's eyes, Kewalram had seen more than just curiosity—he had seen belief. Belief in India's future in the oil industry.

For Kewalram Kanuga, that belief made all the difference.

In the months that followed, Kanuga's vision for Duliajan began to materialize, supported by visits from Central Ministers K.D. Malviya, A.S. Aleggasan, and Humayun Kabir. With approvals from Burmah Oil already secured, the township project advanced rapidly.

Standing on Nehru Maidan, Kanuga reflected on how a twist of fate had brought the Prime Minister to Duliajan. A profound sense of accomplishment washed over him. That one unexpected day had set the township on a path to success.

Kanuga gazed up at the clear sky, a smile spreading across his face. The rain clouds that had once delayed Nehru's arrival now seemed to have, in a way, blessed the future of Duliajan. The township was no longer just an oil hub—it was now a vibrant community, poised to thrive and prosper for generations to come.

Chapter 10:
The Journey of Progress

The developments in Assam were nothing short of revolutionary. One day, as Kewalram Kanuga and S N Viswanath, popularly known as Vish a young geologist, walked through the corridors of the General Office of Duliajan, their conversation turned towards the remarkable feats that had been achieved in recent years.

"Do you remember Vish when we first started laying the pipelines for transporting Assam's crude oil?" Kanuga asked, glancing at the familiar surroundings.

Viswanath smiled. "How could I forget Sir? The challenges seemed insurmountable back then."

Kanuga nodded. "And yet here we are. It's amazing to think that we commissioned the world's first crude oil conditioning plant in 1963."

Viswanath's eyes lit up with pride. "The Upper Assam crude is waxy, thick. Transporting it through a pipeline was almost impossible before that plant. But after those brilliant scientists from BOC successfully conditioned it in the lab and pilot projects, everything changed."

"The plant at Duliajan," Kanuga continued, "built by M/s Whesso Limited from Darlington in the UK, was the first of its kind. We started its construction in 1961 and commissioned it 1963. That plant alone conditioned 8,000 kiloliters of crude oil per day—around two million tons of crude every year. And the best part? Gauhati Refinery began receiving the conditioned crude as soon as it was up and running."

Vishwanath laughed. "I still remember the initial cost estimate Sir — Rs. 1.5 crore. But by the time we were done, it cost Rs. 1.65 crore. Still, it was worth every rupee."

Kanuga smiled. "Yes, it was. And let's not forget the second plant at Moran. Construction started in 1962, and it was commissioned the very next year. By 1964, Oil India Ltd. had two operational plants."

Viswanath shook his head in admiration. "It's hard to believe that just a few years ago, we were struggling to transport waxy crude, and now we've created a system that's not only functional but a world first."

Kanuga's face softened. "We've come a long way, Vish. This pipeline—this conditioning plant—has transformed the landscape of oil transportation in India. And it all started with that crude from Upper Assam."

The two men continued their walk, reflecting on the journey that had led them from impossible challenges to groundbreaking achievements. The Nahorkatiya-Barauni pipeline and the crude oil conditioning plants were more than just feats of engineering; they were symbols of innovation, perseverance, and the indomitable spirit that had come to define the people of Duliajan.

The township of Duliajan had come alive in ways Kewalram Kanuga had always dreamed. The visit from Prime Minister Nehru had given it national attention, and the people of the community felt a sense of pride in being part of something so special. The oil operations were running smoothly, and the township's schools, sports, and cultural programs were flourishing.

The OIL Hospital

The hospital had begun as a modest facility in a C-Type quarter, No. 3, back in 1962. But under Kanuga's guidance, it transformed into a fully functioning medical center, gradually becoming the lifeline for the growing township of Duliajan. By 1964, it was evident that the hospital required further development to meet the healthcare demands of an ever-expanding population.

One afternoon, Kanuga met with Dr. Ratna Kanta Bhuyan, the head of the medical department at Oil India Hospital. As they strolled through the bustling corridors, the air filled with the sounds of patients and medical staff going about their daily routines, the challenges facing the hospital became even more apparent.

"Dr. Bhuyan," Kanuga began, his voice thoughtful as they passed by the small outpatient section, "we've come a long way since this hospital was just a few rooms in a residential quarter. But with Duliajan's population growing so fast, we need to expand—and quickly."

Dr. Bhuyan nodded gravely, his eyes scanning the crowded waiting area. "We've been managing, Sir, but the demand is rising every day. We'll need more space, more doctors, and more specialized services. At this rate, we're still sending patients to Digboi for treatment far too often."

Kanuga smiled reassuringly. "I've already discussed this with the board. We'll allocate the necessary funds to expand the hospital, and we'll do it swiftly. The people of Duliajan deserve the best healthcare we can offer right here, without needing to travel."

The expansion of Oil India Hospital became one of Kanuga's most ambitious projects in the years that followed. By the end of 1964, the construction of a brand-new surgical ward had been completed, enabling more advanced procedures to be performed locally. The addition of a gyno ward followed shortly after, ensuring that the women of the township no longer had to make the arduous journey to Digboi for maternal care.

Kanuga was also instrumental in appointing new doctors. Under his leadership, specialists in pediatrics, surgery, and gynaecology joined the hospital team, reducing the dependency on facilities in Digboi. "We're building a team that can handle anything," Kanuga often remarked to his colleagues, his vision for Duliajan's self-reliance becoming clearer with each passing day.

By 1965, the hospital boasted a surgical theatre equipped with the latest medical technology, several specialized wards, and enough staff to cater to the township's increasing population. Patients who once had to be referred to other towns for even minor surgeries could now receive treatment in Duliajan, thanks to the facility's upgraded infrastructure.

The community began to notice the changes. Families that had once hesitated to leave the familiarity of Digboi now found comfort in Duliajan's growing medical capabilities. Fewer patients were being sent away, and confidence in the local healthcare system flourished.

One evening, as Dr. Bhuyan made his rounds in the new wards, he paused outside the maternity wing, where a newborn's cry echoed softly through the hall. He smiled to himself, thinking of how far they had come. "This," he later told Kanuga over tea, "is the progress we dreamed of."

Kanuga, always modest in the face of success, simply nodded. "It's just the beginning," he said quietly. "Duliajan will continue to grow, and so will this hospital."

By the end of 1967, Duliajan had solidified its place not just as a centre of oil production but as a thriving, self-sufficient township. The people who had once resisted leaving Digboi now proudly called Duliajan home, and the township's growth, both in industry and healthcare, showed no signs of slowing.

Passion for Sports

In Duliajan, Kewalram Kanuga's passion for sports was far more than a pastime. For him, sports served as a way to unite people, encourage teamwork, and uplift the lives of the oil workers and their families. His vision was to create a thriving sports culture in the township, and he had both the influence and dedication to bring it to life.

One evening, as Kewalram sat in his garden sipping tea, he watched his youngest son, Lakshman, practicing swings with his tennis racket in the backyard.

"You know," Kewalram said, watching Lakshman with a proud smile, "we're going to bring some of the finest tennis players in the country right here to Duliajan."

Ganga, his wife, raised an eyebrow. "In this remote place? Who would travel all this way?" she asked, half amused.

Kewalram smiled, a mischievous sparkle in his eye. "Oh, I've got my ways. I've spoken with some friends on the National Tennis Board. Ramanathan Krishnan, Naresh Kumar, Jaideep Mukherjee... even Premjit Lal. They're all coming to play friendly matches with our local players."

Lakshman, overhearing, froze mid-swing. "Wait, Baba, are you serious? They're really coming here?"

Kewalram grinned and nodded. "That's right! And there's more—Thomaz Koch, a Davis Cup player from Brazil, will be here too. Just because we're far from the big cities doesn't mean we can't be part of something bigger."

The news of the event spread swiftly. Soon, the tennis courts were alive with excitement as local players readied themselves to challenge some of the finest. These friendly matches became a celebrated event for the entire township—a moment when Duliajan felt connected to the larger world. Kewalram's vision was beginning to take shape.

But tennis was just the beginning.

Kewalram's dreams reached much further. Football, cricket, badminton, table tennis, even golf—he envisioned them all for Duliajan. "We must strive for excellence in everything," he would often say, overseeing the construction of new sports facilities. He even arranged for professional coaches to visit regularly, ensuring that oil workers, their children, and local talents had access to top-notch training.

Kewalram Kanuga's vision was simple yet profound: Duliajan would be more than just an oil township. It would be a place where sports thrived, where community bonds strengthened, and where residents felt connected—not only to each other but to the world beyond their small town.

One afternoon, as he stood by the newly built football field watching a match between two departmental teams, young engineer Arpan approached him. "Sir, I never imagined we'd have such a setup here in Duliajan. You've transformed this place into something remarkable."

Kanuga smiled, his gaze following the ball as it flew across the field. "It's more than infrastructure, Arpan. It's about giving people something to look forward to, something that brings them together. Teamwork matters, whether on the field or in the oil fields."

The annual sports meets and tournaments soon became a cornerstone of Duliajan's life. These events were celebrated not only for their competitive energy but also for the sense of unity they inspired. Kanuga's dedication to sports reflected his broader vision for the township—a place where people flourished, both professionally and personally.

Thanks to Kewalram Kanuga's unwavering belief in the power of play, sports had become a way of life in Duliajan. One evening, as he and Ganga strolled through the quiet streets, past the school, Nehru Maidan, and the hospital, Ganga turned to him with a gentle smile.

"You've created something incredible here, Kanuga ji. The people, the community—it's everything you envisioned."

He looked at her, his heart full. "It wasn't just me, Ganga. It's everyone who believed in this dream, who came together to make it real."

She nodded, giving his hand a gentle squeeze. "But it all started with your vision. And now, it's come to life."

As they continued their walk, the township lights glowing softly around them, Kewalram felt a deep sense of fulfillment. Duliajan was no longer just an idea or plan —it had become a thriving community. And it would stand as his legacy for generations to come.

Chapter 11:
The Spirit of Community

By the mid-1960s, Duliajan had blossomed into much more than just a township centered around oil production—it had become a lively, close-knit community where life extended well beyond the workplace. Kewalram Kanuga, a key figure in its development, understood that the essence of a flourishing town lay in its power to unite people. To him, sports, entertainment, and culture were vital for nurturing a true sense of togetherness. Driven by this belief, Kanuga set out to create spaces where residents could gather, relax, and celebrate life. His vision gave rise to two of Duliajan's most beloved institutions: the Duliajan Club and the Zaloni Club.

The Creation of Duliajan Club (1962)

Unlike many leaders who might have focused primarily on the needs of officers, Kewalram Kanuga envisioned a more inclusive Duliajan. He recognized that the town's success was built not only by its officers but also by the dedicated men and women who drove its growth—the workers laboring in the oil fields and the staff supporting Oil India's daily operations. For Kanuga, creating a vibrant community meant ensuring that everyone—from top executives to the hard-working employees—had a space to relax, recharge, and feel a sense of belonging.

"We've built homes and schools," Kanuga remarked in a meeting with his team. "But we must also create a space where our workers can relax, enjoy sports, and take part in cultural activities. The Duliajan Club should be a place where everyone feels at home."

Guided by this inclusive vision, Kanuga led the establishment of the Duliajan Club in 1962. Unlike the officer-exclusive Zaloni Club, the Duliajan Club was designed to welcome a broader community—

officers, workers, and the wider township alike. Kanuga envisioned a club where rank and title were set aside, allowing people from all walks of life to gather, share stories, and foster camaraderie in an environment of mutual respect.

The founding of the Duliajan Club marked a significant milestone for the community. In its early days, Kanuga collaborated closely with a diverse team to equip the club with facilities that would serve the varied needs of all its members. This club wasn't merely an afterthought or a symbolic gesture—it was a thoughtful, intentional effort to close the social gap between workers and officers. Kanuga was committed to building a unified township where everyone could find a place to unwind and enjoy some leisure after a hard day's work.

The opening of the Duliajan Club may have been a modest event, but its impact resonated deeply with everyone present. Workers, officers, and their families came together in a rare blending of social circles, standing side by side to celebrate the creation of a space meant for everyone. In his inauguration speech, Kanuga highlighted the importance of community. "This club isn't just for a select few," he said to the crowd. "It's for all of us." The heart of Duliajan isn't only in its oil fields but in its people—the ones who have worked tirelessly to shape this town into what it is today."

At first, the club offered only basic amenities—spaces for social gatherings, small games, and a modest hall for events. But Kanuga, as always, envisioned more. Over time, the Duliajan Club evolved far beyond a simple recreational facility. Situated near the OIL Hospital, it expanded to include a football ground and indoor spaces for table tennis and badminton. The club soon became known not only for sports but also for its vibrant cultural programs, showcasing local talent in music, dance, and drama. It emerged as a true social and cultural hub, where town residents, regardless of their role in the company, could take part in cultural programs, celebrate festivals, and enjoy sporting events together.

The club's welcoming atmosphere nurtured a strong sense of unity within the community. During festivals like Bihu and Durga Puja, the Duliajan Club buzzed with music, dance, and laughter. Workers, many experiencing such events for the first time, now had a platform to showcase their talents, join in performances, and even organize community gatherings. It became a place where cultural traditions were honoured, and where people came together as equals to celebrate their shared heritage.

In those early years, Kanuga was a regular presence at the Duliajan Club. He was often seen talking with workers, inquiring about their families, and discussing ways to improve their lives. "Sir, you've given us more than just a club," one worker remarked to him during a casual conversation. "You've given us a sense of belonging."

Kanuga smiled warmly, his eyes reflecting a deep sense of kindness. "That's the idea," he said. "We're all part of this town. Everyone deserves a place where we can come together, relax, and feel at home."

As the years passed, the Duliajan Club flourished. It became a dynamic hub for a variety of activities—sporting tournaments, cultural nights, family picnics, and even weddings were celebrated within its walls. Workers who once felt distanced from the larger community now had a space where they could build lasting connections, not only with fellow workers but with officers and their families as well. The club stood as a testament to Kanuga's dedication to inclusion, a place where everyone in Duliajan, no matter their rank or status, could unite as one.

Kanuga's vision for the Duliajan Club went beyond offering recreation; it was about creating a space where people felt valued and their contributions to the town's success were acknowledged. By providing workers and their families a place to relax, celebrate, and connect, he cultivated a strong sense of pride within the community. Duliajan wasn't just a place to work—it became a place to live and thrive, largely due to Kanuga's foresight and unwavering commitment to the well-being of everyone.

Today, the Duliajan Club stands as a testament to Kanuga's belief in the strength of community—a lasting symbol of his inclusive vision that united the entire township in a spirit of togetherness and shared purpose.

One sunny Sunday afternoon, Kanuga visited the Duliajan Club, where a friendly cricket match was underway between two local teams. The field sparkled in the sunlight as the crowd cheered and laughed, enjoying the game and the sense of camaraderie it brought. Workers who once felt distant from the social life of Duliajan now had a place where they truly belonged.

As Kanuga watched, a group of workers approached him.

"Sahab, thank you for this club," one said with a smile. "It's brought us all closer. Our children play here, we have a place to relax, and it truly feels like home now."

Kanuga smiled, his heart filled with pride. "This town belongs to all of us," he replied. "And this club is only the beginning. We'll keep building, keep growing—together."

The Formation of Zaloni Club (1968)

The success of the Duliajan Club inspired Kewalram Kanuga to create a similar space, this time specifically for the officers of Oil India. As the company's operations expanded, Kanuga, along with other senior officials, recognized the increasing need for a dedicated space where officers could relax and socialize after their long, demanding workdays. This vision led to the founding of the Zaloni Club, a place designed to foster camaraderie, recreation, and relaxation to flourish.

One afternoon, over a cup of tea, Kewalram Kanuga sat with Mr. Amiya Bhushan Dasgupta, the Field Manager of Oil India Ltd. in Duliajan. Their conversation naturally drifted to the growing number of officers in the township.

"We've built homes, schools, and hospitals," Dasgupta remarked thoughtfully. "But something is still missing, KB. The officers work hard, yet they have no place to relax and unwind."

Kanuga, sensing Dasgupta's intent, smiled and said, "You're thinking of a club for the officers, aren't you?"

Dasgupta nodded, a grin spreading across his face. "Exactly. A space where executives can socialize, unwind, and engage in recreational activities—a place where they can play sports, watch films, enjoy cultural programs, and perhaps share a drink at the bar after a long day. Their well-being is just as vital as the work they do."

Kanuga leaned back thoughtfully, nodding in agreement. "I've been thinking along the same lines, AB. We need a place where they can enjoy tennis, badminton, table tennis, and even host cultural events that bring everyone together."

The vision of creating a space for officers to gather and unwind began to take shape on June 3, 1960, with the temporary inauguration of the Zaloni Club. Initially, it was a modest setup, serving as a simple venue for small get-togethers—a humble beginning but the first step toward something much grander. The temporary club was located at TROCO No. 2, between where bungalows D Plus 156 and 161 now stand— far from the expansive vision Kewalram Kanuga had in mind. As the club's founding President, alongside Brij Mohan Chopra serving as General Secretary, Kanuga was already envisioning something beyond the confines of the temporary setup.

In those early days, the club was simple—just a place for officers to meet, share a cup of tea, and discuss the day's events. The walls might have been plain, the amenities limited, but for Kanuga and the other founding members, it represented something more. It was the seed of a vision that Kanuga carried with him, a vision of a club that would not only serve the officers of Oil India but also become the social and recreational hub of the entire township.

One evening, as Kanuga sat with Chopra and a few other members on the club's verandah, sipping tea and gazing out at the surrounding greenery, he spoke with a spark of excitement in his eyes. "This is just the beginning," he said. "One day, this club will have facilities that rival those of any major city—tennis courts, swimming pools, everything."

Chopra smiled, "Swimming pools in Duliajan? Now that's something I'd like to see."

"You'll see it, Brij," Kanuga replied with confidence. "We're not just building a club; we're building a community."

As the years passed, that dream remained firmly in Kanuga's mind. Every detail, every plan for the new, permanent Zaloni Club, was carefully considered. He envisioned a place where officers and their families could not only socialize but also engage in sports, celebrate milestones, and find a true sense of belonging in the growing township.

By 1968, Kanuga's vision began to take shape. The Zaloni Club's permanent premises, located near the scenic golf course, were completed. On December 23, 1968, the new location was officially inaugurated by Major General Raja in a grand ceremony attended by officers, their families, and dignitaries from across the region.

The club's new structure surpassed all of Kanuga's expectations. It was more than just a building; it symbolized Duliajan's growth and stood as a testament to the hard work and dedication of the Oil India community. The club now featured an array of top-tier facilities that Kanuga had dreamed of in the early years. There were tennis courts where officers could unwind with a game after work, and a badminton hall that quickly became home to regular tournaments. However, the highlight was the addition of a swimming pool—the first in the township and a source of immense pride for everyone involved.

"Brij, do you remember when you laughed at the idea of a swimming pool?" Kanuga joked one afternoon as they stood by the newly built pool, watching children splash around.

Chopra grinned and clapped him on the shoulder. "I stand corrected, my friend. You've truly built something remarkable here."

The Zaloni Club soon became more than just a place for sports. It transformed into a vibrant space where officers and their families could come together for a variety of activities. Table tennis quickly became a favorite pastime, with officers often staying late into the evening for friendly yet competitive matches. The club was not only a recreational hub—it became a place where lifelong friendships were formed, where officers bonded over shared experiences, and where families could relax and enjoy leisure time in a space that felt like home.

The Zaloni Club became a symbol of progress, not only for Oil India but for Duliajan as a whole. Named after the Zaloni Tea Estate, the club featured state-of-the-art amenities, including sporting facilities, a bar, an auditorium, and a spacious area for cultural programs. Kanuga had realized his vision, creating a center that served the social and recreational needs of the community, bringing people from all walks of life together. Over time, the club became renowned not only for its sports offerings but also for the cultural events it hosted—from festivals to officer gatherings—all at the heart of this growing township.

For Kanuga, watching the club come to life was one of his proudest accomplishments. It was more than just bricks and mortar—it represented the fulfillment of a promise to the officers and their families: a promise of community, recreation, and shared joy. As he walked through the club, seeing children play and officers laughing over a game of tennis or table tennis, he realized that the Zaloni Club was more than a dream. It had become a legacy, one that would endure for generations to come.

Cultural programs quickly became a defining feature of the Zaloni Club. A passionate admirer of the arts, Kanuga made sure the club hosted a diverse range of events, including musical performances, theater productions, and traditional Assamese dance shows. These gatherings fostered a deep sense of community among officers and their families, with evenings filled with music, dance, and shared laughter.

One evening, Kewalram and his wife, Ganga, attended a vibrant cultural night at the Zaloni Club. As they watched a group of performers in dazzling costumes bring traditional Assamese dance to life, the rhythmic beats and graceful movements mesmerized the audience. The applause at the end was thunderous, a clear sign of how much these events meant to the residents.

Ganga leaned in toward Kewalram, her eyes sparkling with contentment. "This is exactly what Duliajan needed," she whispered. "It feels like home now, filled with so much joy and togetherness."

Kewalram nodded, a deep sense of pride swelling within him. "Yes, this is what a community is all about—bringing people together, sharing experiences, and celebrating our culture."

As the years passed, both the Duliajan Club and the Zaloni Club came to embody the soul of Duliajan's growing identity and sense of community. The sports facilities, from the tennis courts to the swimming pool, became cherished venues for relaxation and healthy competition, while the cultural events breathed life into the township, forging connections that extended beyond the workplace.

Kanuga's vision was clear: he didn't just want to build a functional township for Oil India's employees; he wanted to create a thriving, united home for everyone. The Zaloni Club, with its blend of sports, culture, and fellowship, stood as a testament to that vision, nurturing not just the bodies but also the spirits of the officers and their families. It was more than just a club—it became the heartbeat of the community, a place where lifelong memories were made, and where Duliajan truly became a home for all.

Cultural Programs: A Common Thread

The Zaloni Club and Duliajan Club became vibrant hubs of cultural activity in Duliajan, hosting regular events that highlighted the rich heritage of Assam and beyond. Under the visionary leadership of K.B. Kanuga, who firmly believed in the power of art to unite communities, these clubs became much more than recreational venues. They transformed into platforms for celebrating and preserving the rich heritage of Assam and beyond.

In 1965, the Duliajan Club organized its first major cultural festival, bringing together musicians, dancers, and performers from across the region. Families from all over Duliajan gathered to celebrate, creating a vibrant and joyous atmosphere. The event was a tremendous success, leaving a lasting impression on the community.

As the festival came to an end, K.B. Kanuga stepped onto the stage to address the crowd.

"This township was built by all of you," he began, his voice steady and filled with pride. "These clubs, these events—they exist for you. Duliajan is not just a place to work; it is a place to live, to grow, and to celebrate life together. I am proud to call this community my home, and I hope each of you feels the same."

The crowd erupted in applause, and in that moment, Kewalram Kanuga knew that Duliajan had become everything he had envisioned—and more.

By the mid-1960s, the Zaloni Club and Duliajan Club had firmly established themselves as integral to the township's social life. Both officers and workers came together in these spaces to relax and immerse themselves in the vibrant cultural offerings of the community. Through these clubs, Kanuga's dream of fostering a connected and thriving community had come to life.

As the sun set on another lively evening at the clubs, the air buzzed with laughter and music. Kanuga stood quietly, gazing over the bustling town, his heart brimming with fulfillment. Duliajan had transformed from a mere industrial township into a vibrant, living community filled with joy, culture, and spirit.

Kewalram Kanuga was more than a man of oil and industry—he was a lover of music, particularly the folk melodies of his Sindhi heritage. Known for his boundless enthusiasm, he often infused social gatherings with energy by singing old Sindhi folk songs. His hearty laughter, rhythmic clapping, and foot-tapping brought a celebratory warmth to every occasion, leaving everyone around him uplifted.

One evening, during a grand event at the Duliajan Club, the air was thick with excitement. The legendary Dr. Bhupen Hazarika was set to perform, and the crowd eagerly awaited his arrival. Among them was Kewalram Kanuga, brimming with anticipation. He had always admired Hazarika's extraordinary talent for capturing the essence of Assam—its rivers, mountains, and people—through his soulful music.

As Bhupen Hazarika's rich, soulful voice filled the air, Kewalram Kanuga sat spellbound, fully immersed in the magic of the performance. But the evening held an unexpected twist.

Midway through the concert, Hazarika paused, his warm smile spreading as he scanned the crowd. "There's someone here tonight," he began, "whose voice carries the essence of the land. I've heard he can bring the spirit of his people alive with just a clap and a song."

The audience murmured in curiosity as Hazarika's gaze settled on Kewalram in the front row. "Kewalramji," he said with a twinkle in his eye, "will you join me on stage?"

Cheers erupted from the audience, urging Kanuga forward. Flustered yet excited, he stood, his broad smile revealing both nerves and delight. As he approached the stage, Hazarika placed a reassuring hand on his shoulder. "Let's show them," he said warmly, "what it means to make music from the heart."

Kewalram took a deep breath, allowing the familiar rhythms of his childhood to flow through him. As the music began, he and Hazarika created something extraordinary—melting the folk tunes of Assam with those of Sindh. Hazarika's deep, melodic voice harmonized beautifully with Kanuga's spirited clapping and foot-tapping, transforming the stage into a vibrant celebration of cultural unity.

The audience sat spellbound, their amazement quickly turning into participation as Kanuga's infectious energy spread through the room. Soon, everyone was clapping along, carried by the sheer joy of the performance. When the song ended, the room erupted in thunderous applause.

Bhupen Hazarika turned to Kanuga with a warm smile and embraced him. "You've got the soul of an artist, Kewalramji," he said, his voice filled with genuine admiration. "It was an honor to share the stage with you."

Still catching his breath, Kanuga laughed heartily. "The honor was all mine, Bhupenda. This is a moment I'll cherish forever."

But their collaboration didn't end there. At Kanuga's invitation, Bhupen Hazarika brought a team of renowned artists from Mumbai to Duliajan for the next cultural evening at the club. The event featured legends like Talat Mahmood and Daisy Irani, creating a spectacle the small town had never witnessed before. The credit for this extraordinary gathering of talent belonged entirely to Kewalram Kanuga.

For Kanuga, music was far more than mere entertainment—it was a bridge between cultures, a means of connecting people. Whether singing folk tunes with friends or sharing a stage with iconic artists, he believed in music's ability to bring joy, foster unity, and create unforgettable memories. And that night in Duliajan, with Bhupen

Hazarika by his side, Kanuga's passion for music shone as brilliantly as his leadership in the oil fields.

Oily Kanuga's Wily Performance

Kewalram Kanuga was not only a visionary leader in the oil industry—he was a man deeply passionate about sports. Whether it was cricket, football, or tennis, he firmly believed in the power of sports to build team spirit and camaraderie. His enthusiasm for the game often drew him to the field, particularly during inter-departmental matches in Duliajan and regional tournaments.

One afternoon, the Duliajan Club faced their toughest challenge yet—a high-stakes cricket match against the Shillong Club. The atmosphere was electric, brimming with excitement and tension. As the game approached its thrilling climax, Shillong needed just two runs to secure victory, while Duliajan had three wickets left to claim.

Kewalram stood fielding near the boundary line, his eyes fixed on the action as the pressure intensified. Sensing the mounting tension, the team captain, visibly anxious, turned to him and said, "KB, they're on the verge of winning. We need a miracle."

With his trademark calm, Kewalram picked up the ball and said, "Let's see if we can spin our way out of this."

The fielders quickly took their positions as Kewalram prepared to bowl. His first delivery was a masterfully spun ball, drifting deceptively toward the batsman, who prepared for what seemed like an easy shot. But as the ball approached, it spun sharply, catching the batsman off-guard. He swung wildly but missed by inches. The wicketkeeper, sharp and alert, snapped off the bails in an instant, catching the batsman out of his crease—stumped!

The crowd roared with excitement as Duliajan secured their first wicket, but the match was still hanging in the balance. The next batsman stepped onto the pitch with confidence in his stride, needing only two runs to clinch victory.

Kewalram's second delivery was just as deceptive. The ball dipped sharply as it reached the batsman, enticing him into a risky drive. The bat connected, but the ball flew higher than intended. The crowd held its breath as it soared through the air, appearing for a moment as though it might clear the fielders. But a teammate at mid-off, perfectly positioned, sprinted forward and made a stunning catch just inches from the ground. Another wicket fell.

The atmosphere was electric, with excitement and tension filling the air. The scoreboard still showed just two runs needed, but Duliajan had taken two quick wickets, With each passing moment, the tension continued to rise.

The final batsman stepped onto the crease, and the match hung by a thread. All eyes turned to Kewalram as he prepared for the decisive delivery. He paused, the weight of the moment heavy on his shoulders, then unleashed his most deceptive spin yet.

The batsman hesitated, uncertain of the ball's trajectory. He swung defensively, but the ball spun sharply away, grazing the edge of his bat. The wicketkeeper, diving to his left with impeccable reflexes, stretched out his gloves and secured a spectacular catch. The game was over.

The Duliajan crowd erupted in sheer joy and disbelief. Kewalram had delivered a flawless over, achieving a miraculous victory when all seemed lost. His teammates rushed to him, hoisting him onto their shoulders in a triumphant celebration.

The next morning, the Shillong Times ran the headline: "Oily Kanuga's Wily Performance," applauding Kewalram's brilliant spin bowling that had turned the game in the thrilling final over.

Later that evening, as the team gathered to celebrate, a young player looked at Kewalram with admiration and said, "That was incredible, sir! You've still got it."

Kanuga smiled and shook his head. "It's not about age," he said, a twinkle in his eye. "It's about believing in the game, trusting your team, and remembering that until the last ball is bowled, anything is possible."

For Kewalram Kanuga, sports were never just about competition. They were a means to unite people, inspire them to surpass their limits, and demonstrate that with heart, determination, and teamwork, even the impossible could be achieved. Whether on the cricket field or in the oil fields, Kewalram Kanuga's indomitable spirit remained a source of inspiration for everyone fortunate enough to be part of his journey.

Chapter 12:
The Legacy of Education

By the mid-1960s, Duliajan had evolved from a bustling oil town into a vibrant and thriving community. What had once been a hub for exploration and production had grown into a place where families settled, children thrived, and dreams took flight. For Kewalram Kanuga, the heart of this transformation was perfectly symbolized by the Oil India Higher Secondary School.

From its inception in 1963, the Oil India Higher Secondary School became a beacon of hope and opportunity for the children of the township. In its early days, before its permanent building was completed, the school operated out of the Duliajan Club. Once a hub of social gatherings for oil executives, the club now resonated with the sounds of lessons, laughter, and the promise of a brighter future as it temporarily served as a space to nurture young minds.

Kanuga firmly believed that education was the foundation of a strong community, and he ensured that his own children were no exception to this principle. His children attended schools and colleges across Assam, and their academic achievements brought him immense pride and satisfaction.

On a warm evening in 1965, Kewalram Kanuga and his wife, Ganga, sat together on their porch, watching the children returning from school. Ganga's face lit up with a gentle smile, her eyes filled with contentment. "The children of Duliajan are truly fortunate," she said softly. "They've been given the opportunity to study at one of the finest schools in the region."

Kewalram nodded, his heart filled with pride. "It's more than just fortune," he said. "It's the result of hard work from everyone in this township. Together, we've built something enduring—something that will shape not only our children but future generations as well."

Their youngest son, Lakshman, one of the school's first batch of students, approached them with his books in hand. Sitting down beside them, he said, "Baba, I've been thinking a lot about my future."

Kewalram smiled, recognizing the seriousness in his son's expression. "What's on your mind, Lakshman?" he asked gently.

Lakshman replied earnestly, "I want to make something meaningful out of my studies. I enjoy the Arts stream, but I want to excel. My goal is to be among Assam's top rank holders in the Higher Secondary Examination."

Kewalram's eyes sparkled with pride. "You have the drive, Lakshman. With your determination, there's nothing you can't achieve," he said confidently.

Ganga placed a comforting hand on Lakshman's shoulder. "We believe in you, Lakshman. You carry the same passion as your father, and with that, whatever path you choose, success will surely follow."

By 1967, as the Higher Secondary examinations approached, Lakshman's teachers were confident in his ability to excel. One afternoon, just days before the results were due, Kewalram spotted his son sitting under a tree, a book resting in his hands.

"Nervous about the results?" Kewalram asked as he sat down beside Lakshman.

Lakshman offered a small smile, though the flicker of anxiety in his eyes was unmistakable. "A little," he admitted. "I've worked hard, but there's always that uncertainty."

Kewalram smiled warmly, his voice steady with reassurance. "I've seen the dedication you've put into your studies. That kind of hard work never goes unnoticed. Whatever the outcome, remember—I'm proud of you."

A few days later, Duliajan was alive with excitement. The results were out—Lakshman had not only passed with distinction but had also secured the top rank in the Arts stream across the entire state of Assam. His remarkable achievement was closely followed by Saryu Tripathi, who earned the third rank in the Science stream. The news spread like wildfire, and soon the entire township was celebrating the success of its young scholars.

For Kewalram, this was more than just a personal triumph; it was the realization of his vision for Duliajan—a township where young minds could learn, grow, and thrive. The Oil India Higher Secondary School, once a modest institution, had now earned a reputation for producing some of the brightest talents in Assam.

That evening, as the celebrations settled and calm returned, Lakshman sat with his family, the joy of his achievement still fresh. Turning to his father with heartfelt gratitude, he said softly, "Baba, I couldn't have done this without you. You built this town, this school—you gave us all a chance."

Kewalram smiled, his pride unmistakable. "No, son. This is your achievement. It's your hard work and dedication that brought you here. I merely helped lay the foundation."

Beside him, Ganga wiped a tear from her eye. "We're so proud of you, Lakshman. You've not only made us proud but this entire township as well."

As news of Lakshman and Saryu's achievements spread, Duliajan swelled with pride. These milestones were more than individual victories—they were triumphs for the entire community. The Oil India Higher Secondary School had become a symbol of excellence, inspiring students across the township to dream bigger and aim higher.

In the weeks that followed, the school buzzed with a renewed sense of purpose. Teachers pushed their students to strive for greater heights, parents encouraged their children to follow in Lakshman and Saryu's footsteps, and the entire township felt the ripple effect of their success. The school had transformed into more than just an institution—it was now a shining beacon of educational excellence in Assam.

One afternoon, as Kewalram strolled through the school grounds, the headmaster, Mr. Hare Krishna Das, approached him with a warm and enthusiastic handshake.

"Kanuga Sir," Das began, his voice filled with admiration, "Lakshman and Saryu's achievements have brought immense honor to this school. Your vision has truly transformed this place."

Kewalram smiled modestly. "The credit belongs to the students, Mr. Das. But yes, I'm proud of what we've all built together."

Das nodded in agreement. "This school has become a beacon of hope for so many children. You've truly changed lives, Sir."

For Kewalram, Lakshman's achievement was profoundly personal. It marked the fulfillment of his dream to see Duliajan become more than just an industrial hub. Surrounded by the students who had brought his vision to life, he felt an overwhelming sense of triumph.

That evening, as the sun set over Duliajan, Kewalram stood on his porch with Ganga by his side. Together, they watched the twinkling lights of the township they had helped build, confident that the future of Duliajan—its families and children—was in good hands.

Chapter 13:
A Community's Growth

Mr. John Campbell Finlay served as the first Managing Director of Oil India Ltd. from 1962 to 1969. A visionary leader, Finlay played a pivotal role in laying the company's early foundations. His leadership extended beyond corporate offices as he frequently visited Duliajan during Kewalram Kanuga's tenure. These visits allowed him to personally oversee the development of both the township and the oil fields, contributing significantly to the community's growth.

One afternoon, as Kanuga discussed the township's expansion with Mr. Gowan, Finlay arrived in Duliajan for one of his visits. The two men greeted him warmly.

"John, welcome!" Kanuga said with a smile, shaking his hand.

Finlay, ever the hands-on leader, wasted no time. "It's wonderful to see how this place is shaping up. You've done remarkable work here, KB," he said, his Scottish accent still pronounced despite years in India. "But we need to ensure this isn't just a company built of bricks and steel. The work culture we establish will be the lifeblood of Oil India for generations to come."

Kanuga nodded in agreement, fully aligned with Finlay's vision. "I couldn't agree more, John. We're not just focusing on infrastructure; we're committed to fostering a sense of belonging among the people."

Finlay's sharp blue eyes swept over the bustling township, now alive with activity. "Good. It's the people who matter most. If we take care of them, Oil India will flourish. What we build today will become the lifeblood of this company for generations to come."

Under Finlay's leadership, Oil India developed a culture defined by a strong work ethic and a deep sense of responsibility. His visits to Duliajan were far more than routine; they were purposeful opportunities to mentor and guide. Through his efforts, the values of dedication, safety, and respect for the workforce became enduring pillars of the company's identity.

As Kanuga and Finlay walked through the township, pausing at a work site, Finlay turned to Kanuga and said, "You know, KB, we're not just drilling wells and constructing a townships here. We're building a legacy. Years from now, this place will be the heart of Oil India, and the culture we establish today will be its lifeblood."

Kanuga smiled, nodding in agreement. "That's precisely what we're striving for. And with leaders like you guiding us, I'm confident we're on the right path."

Finlay's visionary contributions influenced every aspect of Oil India's operations, from implementing robust safety protocols to cultivating a sense of ownership among the workforce. His enduring legacy continues to shape the company, where the principles he championed—hard work, unity, and community pride—remain vital to its identity today.

In its early days, Oil India was eager to carve out an identity distinct from the well-established operations at Digboi. Establishing a new township near the heart of oilfield activity became an inevitable step. The search for a suitable location proved surprisingly straightforward. A vast tract of land with favorable natural features, close to the Duliajan railway station, was identified. This land, primarily part of the Zaloni Tea Estate, was acquired with minimal effort, as negotiations involved only a single owner.

Under Kanuga's visionary leadership, Oil India reached a significant milestone that enhanced its stature in the global oil and gas industry. In 1964, Duliajan was chosen to host the International Geological Congress, a prestigious event that brought together the world's leading geologists. This moment was a unique opportunity for both Oil India and Assam, showcasing the region's oil-rich landscapes to top experts from around the globe.

As preparations began, Kanuga's dynamic energy radiated throughout Duliajan. He was determined that every detail would showcase Oil India's pride, potential, and Assam's renowned hospitality. "We're not just hosting an event; we're welcoming the world," he reminded his team, highlighting the significance of the occasion. The township, nurtured under his meticulous leadership, buzzed with excitement as his team worked diligently to ensure every visitor felt truly at home.

The congress was led by Percy Evans, a towering figure in geology whose research had greatly advanced the understanding of Assam's oil and mineral reserves. Evans arrived in Duliajan with his wife and was welcomed in true Assamese tradition. Kanuga personally greeted them at the Mohanbari airstrip, presenting a traditional gamosa and a bouquet of local flowers as symbols of respect and hospitality. With warmth and pride, he introduced the Evanses to the unique charm of Assam, offering them a glimpse into the culture he held so dearly.

Over the following days, Kanuga ensured that the Evanses and other international delegates experienced both the impactful work of Oil India and the stunning landscapes that had become Kanuga's own field of exploration and dedication. Guided tours of the oil fields were arranged, allowing Percy Evans and other leading geologists to witness firsthand the vastness and richness of the region's oil reserves.

"Mr. Kanuga, I must say, I'm thoroughly impressed," Evans remarked one evening over dinner. "The progress Oil India has achieved here, in such challenging terrain, is truly remarkable. You've accomplished something extraordinary."

Kanuga smiled, a sense of pride evident in his expression. "Thank you, Sir. We've faced our share of challenges, but I firmly believe Assam's potential is boundless. And the team here—they are as dedicated as they come."

Seated beside Ganga, Mrs. Evans expressed her admiration for the township. "It's so peaceful here, Ganga. There's a wonderful sense of community that's rare to find," she said warmly.

Ganga, ever gracious, replied with a gentle smile, "That's all thanks to Kanuga ji. He's always believed in building more than just an industry. For him, this is home, and he wants everyone here to feel the same way."

The congress was a resounding success, characterized by insightful technical discussions, engaging field visits, and a spirit of mutual respect that transcended cultural boundaries. The delegates returned to their countries with tales of Assam's oil-rich lands and the warmth of its people, leaving a lasting impression on Oil India's global reputation.

The congress remained a cherished memory for Kanuga, a moment when Duliajan truly opened its doors to the world. Under his leadership, Oil India emerged not only as an industrial powerhouse but also as a place defined by warmth, community, and ambition.

Kewalram Kanuga often reminisced about the early days of Duliajan, a time when the land was wild and untamed. One evening, as he sat in his office with his junior colleague Jagannathan, he shared his memories.

"When we first started clearing this area," he began, his voice carrying a mix of pride and nostalgia, "it was nothing but dense bushland. The challenges we faced weren't just about the terrain. There were real dangers—wildlife roamed freely. In those early days, we had to deal with four leopards and two tigers just to make the place safe enough to work. What you see today in Duliajan truly emerged from nothing."

Jagannathan leaned forward, captivated by Kanuga's words as he tried to envision the untamed wilderness he was describing. It was almost impossible to reconcile the thriving township he saw today with the wild, dangerous landscape of the past.

"It's incredible," he said thoughtfully. "To think that, despite how rough it must have been in the beginning, you've managed to build all of this."

Kanuga smiled, his eyes glimmering with a blend of pride and nostalgia. "It wasn't just about oil, Jag," he said. "From the very beginning, we understood that drilling wells and laying pipelines wouldn't be enough. If we wanted to build something enduring—something that would draw people here and make them stay—we needed more than infrastructure. We needed schools, hospitals, parks—places where families could grow and thrive. We needed a real community."

Transforming the dense jungle into a liveable township was a monumental task. Faced with this enormous challenge, the planners prioritised simplicity over grandeur. They designed five basic types of sturdies, functional bungalows to house employees and their families. The township spanned 590 acres, with wide roads lined by flowering trees, parks for children to play in, and communal spaces for gatherings. Local industries were also encouraged—brick manufacturing, for instance, was supported with natural gas supplied by the company to private kilns, fostering growth as Duliajan expanded.

"Of course, our first priority was always the operational side," Kanuga said, his tone shifting to a more businesslike demeanour. "We had to build the industrial area, spread over 131 acres, along with office buildings, a water treatment plant, and everything necessary to keep the oil flowing. But we didn't stop there. By 1961, the OIL Market was established. In 1962, the Duliajan Club was ready, followed by the Zaloni Club in 1964. Finally, the general office, as you know, was completed by 1968."

Jagannathan smiled, reflecting on his own early days with Oil India. "You haven't just carved a township out of the jungle, KB," he said warmly. "You've created something truly remarkable."

Kanuga nodded thoughtfully. "But there was one more thing we needed—a name. Zaloni was a beautiful choice, but it would have caused confusion with the nearby tea estate. After some discussion, we settled on Duliajan, named after the nearby railway station."

Jagannathan raised an eyebrow, intrigued. "I've heard a few different stories about how Duliajan got its name. What's the real one?"

Kanuga smiled softly, savoring the moment. "There are always stories, but the one I find most believable is that this area was once a camp for the Dulias—the palanquin bearers of the Ahom nobles who passed through here. The 'jan' part likely refers to the small stream that flows nearby. It fits, doesn't it? There's even a village called Duliagaon just west of the railway track, right across from the industrial area."

The two men sat quietly for a moment, absorbing the weight of history. From its humble beginnings, when the land was little more than overgrown tea estate fields, to the bustling township it had become, Duliajan wasn't just a place—it was a testament to what vision, hard work, and determination could accomplish.

Breaking the silence, Jagannathan said thoughtfully, "It's incredible to think about, KB. Duliajan isn't just an industrial hub anymore. It's a living, breathing community."

Kanuga smiled, his expression filled with deep satisfaction. "Exactly. That's what makes it all worthwhile. It's no longer just about the oil anymore—it's about the people. We've created a place where families can grow, children can dream, and lives can take shape. That's the true legacy of Duliajan."

As the evening deepened, the two men drove through the township, taking in its quiet vitality. The cheerful sounds of children playing in open fields, the faint hum of machinery from the industrial area, and the cool breeze carrying the fragrance of flowering trees all spoke to the transformation of this once untamed land.

For Kanuga, Duliajan was no longer just a network of wells, pipelines, and buildings. It had grown into a thriving, vibrant community. And in that, he found his deepest pride."This place we built," he said softly, almost as if speaking to himself, "is about so much more than just oil now." It's about the lives we've touched and the futures we've shaped. That's what makes it all worthwhile."

By the close of the 1960s, Duliajan had flourished into a bustling township filled with life and opportunity. Kewalram Kanuga, who had played a key role in its creation and growth, now watched as the town expanded beyond his original vision. With the success of the Oil Higher Secondary School and the sense of belonging fostered by the Zaloni Club and Duliajan Club, Duliajan had become more than just a workplace—it had become a place where families could truly thrive.

The success of Lakshman and Saryu, who topped the Higher Secondary examination in Assam, had sparked inspiration among the youth of Duliajan. Education had become the cornerstone of the town's growth, with parents encouraging their children to study diligently, dream ambitiously, and aspire to build a future beyond the oil fields.

One afternoon, Kanuga visited the school, now a proud symbol of the township's progress. As he strolled through the familiar halls, students and teachers greeted him warmly, fully aware of the pivotal role he had played in shaping their futures. Walking beside him was Mr. Hare Krishna Das, the headmaster, who reflected on the school's remarkable growth.

"The students are more motivated than ever, Kanuga Sir," Das said with a smile. "Lakshman and Saryu's success has set a benchmark that many are now striving to reach. It's remarkable how far the school has grown in such a short time."

Kanuga nodded, his gaze lingering on the bustling classrooms. "It's not just about excelling in exams. It's about giving these children the opportunity to realize their potential. I'm proud of what we've built here, but there's always more to be done."

Das's smile deepened. "The foundation you've laid has already transformed countless lives. These students will go on to shape the future of Assam—and beyond."

As the township flourished, so did its social and cultural life. The Zaloni Club became a vibrant hub for officers and their families, hosting everything from sports tournaments to cultural programs.

Meanwhile, the Duliajan Club served as a center of entertainment and connection for workers and the larger community, fostering a sense of unity in the growing town.

KB Kanuga, a firm believer in creating spaces where people could come together, often attended events at both clubs. One evening, during a cultural night at the Zaloni Club, he and Ganga enjoyed a lively performance of traditional Assamese music and dance. The club was alive with energy, filled with families, officers, and their children, all reveling in the vibrant celebration of local culture.

As the night progressed, Mr. Gowan, who had traveled from Digboi to attend the program, approached Kanuga with a glass of whisky in hand, his face glowing with satisfaction.

"KB," Gowan said with a warm smile, "you've outdone yourself again. The Zaloni Club has truly become the heart of the officers' community."

Kanuga returned the smile. "It's not just my doing, Gowan. The officers of Oil India Ltd and their families have shaped it into what it is today."

Gowan raised his glass in a toast. "To the officers of OIL—and to you, KB. You haven't just built a township; you've built a legacy."

By 1968, Duliajan had emerged as a model township for the region. Oil India Limited's operations were running smoothly, and the company's success was reflected in the vibrant community that had grown around it. Yet, even as the town flourished, Kanuga remained focused on the challenges ahead.

One of the most pressing concerns was the expansion of oil operations. As Oil India ventured deeper into the fields at Naharkatiya, Moran, and Hoogrijan, the need for skilled workers and engineers grew significantly. Kanuga collaborated closely with the management to ensure the township could support this growing workforce. He prioritized providing adequate housing, quality education, and reliable healthcare, ensuring that both employees and their families had everything they needed to thrive.

One afternoon in 1968, during a meeting with the Oil India board, the discussion turned to the company's future expansion. Mr. John Finlay, the Managing Director, reviewed the figures in front of him and said, "We're seeing increased production at both Naharkatiya and Moran."

Kanuga leaned forward. "But with that growth comes the need for more infrastructure. We'll have to build additional housing, expand the school, and possibly even the hospital. And we need a college so that the students passing out from the school can pursue higher studies right here in Duliajan "

Finlay nodded thoughtfully. "You're right. We've built a strong foundation, but we can't afford to become complacent. The township has to grow alongside the operations. If we don't provide for the people, we risk losing everything we've worked so hard to build."

The board members murmured in agreement, acknowledging the importance of Kanuga's vision. Recognizing his dedication to Duliajan and his tireless efforts, the board made a significant decision during that very meeting: they promoted K.B. Kanuga to Resident Director of Oil India Ltd. in Duliajan. It was a well-earned acknowledgment of his leadership and commitment.

Kanuga's new role was more than just a title—it was a call to action. With increased responsibility and influence, he worked relentlessly to drive progress. By 1969, his vision became a reality with the establishment of Duliajan College, fulfilling his dream of providing higher education opportunities within the township and ensuring a brighter future for the community.

Chapter 14:
The Battle for Life

In 1966, the house in Duliajan was alive with joy and celebration as Kewalram and Ganga prepared for the grand wedding of their eldest daughter, Mira. She was marrying Hiroo, a Drilling Engineer with Assam Oil. The event was a magnificent affair, filled with laughter, love, and the vibrant presence of relatives and friends who had gathered from far and wide. The air was heavy with the sweet fragrance of flowers and the warmth of the family. In the days leading up to the wedding, Kewalram and Ganga were swept up in a whirlwind of ceremonies, preparations, and precious moments, barely finding a moment to catch their breath.

After the final outstation guest had departed, the house felt noticeably different. The lively laughter and music had faded, giving way to a calm stillness, though the warmth of the celebration still lingered in the corners of their home. Life seemed to be settling back into its familiar rhythm—or so they thought.

Just a few days later, as Ganga busied herself tidying up the last traces of the festivities, she was suddenly overcome by a strange dizziness. She reached out to steady herself against a chair, blinking rapidly in an attempt to clear her vision, but the room continued to spin. Her body grew unnervingly heavy, and before she could call out for help, darkness enveloped her.

Kewalram was in the next room when he heard the sudden, unmistakable thud of something hitting the floor. Alarmed, he rushed in to find Ganga lying motionless on the ground. His heart raced, a wave of fear gripping him as he dropped to his knees beside her.

"Ganga? Ganga!" he called out, his voice thick with panic. He gently shook her, repeating her name with growing desperation, but there was no response.

Kewalram, usually the epitome of calm and composure, felt panic tightening its grip on him. His hands trembled as he fumbled to check for a pulse, the world around him blurring into a surreal haze. It felt like a nightmare—one he couldn't escape.

Within minutes, Dr. R.K. Bhuyan, the Chief Medical Officer of the Duliajan hospital, arrived with his deputy, Dr. J.C. Laskar. Without hesitation, they sprang into action, their faces etched with focus. Kewalram stood nearby, helpless and heartbroken, watching them work tirelessly to stabilize Ganga. He tried to maintain his composure, but inside, he was unraveling. The love of his life, his anchor and strength, lay unresponsive, and there was nothing he could do.

After what seemed like an eternity, Dr. Bhuyan turned to Kewalram, His expression was serious, his voice calm but laced with concern. "She needs more advanced care. We have to transfer her to Digboi immediately."

Kewalram swallowed hard, his thoughts racing. "Do whatever it takes, doctor," he said, his voice quivering. "Just… save her, please."

News of Ganga's condition reached John Watt, the CEO of Assam Oil, who quickly stepped in to offer assistance. "We can move her to the AOC hospital in Digboi," he suggested. "It's better equipped, and we can fly in specialists from Calcutta."

Within hours, Ganga was transported to the Digboi hospital. Specialists from Calcutta arrived promptly and began assessing her condition, but despite their efforts, she remained in a coma.

Kewalram stayed by her bedside, holding her hand as waves of worry washed over him. His voice, heavy with emotion, broke as he whispered to her, "You'll get through this, Ganga. I know you will. Please… don't leave me."

Each night, he refused to leave her side. Though his eyes were heavy with exhaustion, his heart wouldn't allow him to let go. He often sat there, gazing at her peaceful face, willing her to wake up, praying for a miracle to bring her back to him.

Meanwhile, Word of Ganga's illness quickly spread through the community, sparking an incredible outpouring of support. Neighbors, friends, and even those who barely knew the family came forward to help in whatever way they could. Mrs. Shobhana Ranade, a devout follower of Vinoba Bhave, organized special poojas for Ganga's recovery. Prayer meetings were held in temples, gurdwaras, and churches across Duliajan and beyond, uniting people of all faiths in their hope for her healing.

One evening, as Kewalram sat quietly in the hospital, a well-wisher approached him. Their voice was gentle, their eyes filled with sympathy. "We've arranged a prayer meeting at the temple tonight," they said. "Everyone is praying for her recovery."

Kewalram's eyes filled with tears. Overcome with emotion, he nodded and whispered, "Thank you." The kindness and solidarity of the community gave him strength in his darkest moments, reminding him that he wasn't alone in his prayers for Ganga.

Days turned into weeks, and Ganga remained in a coma. Though Kewalram never showed it, hope was beginning to slip from his grasp. Yet, he refused to give up entirely.

One quiet afternoon, as he sat by her bedside, holding her hand as he had done countless times before, he suddenly felt her fingers twitch. He froze, unsure if it was real or his imagination playing tricks on him. Then, her eyelids fluttered open.

"Ganga?" he whispered, his voice trembling with disbelief and hope.

Her eyes slowly focused on him, and though she was weak, a faint smile appeared on her lips.

and though she was weak, a faint smile appeared on her lips.

"You're back," Kewalram choked out, gripping her hand tightly as tears streamed down his face. Relief, love, and gratitude overwhelmed him. After all the prayers and sleepless nights, she was here—awake and with him again. It was the moment he had been waiting for, the miracle he had prayed for.

Ganga's recovery was slow and demanding, but she had overcome the worst. Back in Duliajan, Dr. Laskar took charge of her rehabilitation, visiting regularly to monitor her progress. Dr. Dutta from Digboi also checked in periodically to ensure her recovery stayed on track. Step by step, with unwavering determination and the support of those around her, Ganga began her journey toward healing.

Kewalram, steadfast in his devotion, refused to leave Ganga's side and vowed to assist in every way he could. He eagerly learned the basics of physiotherapy, practicing the exercises so he could help her daily. Sitting beside her, he would gently guide her movements, his voice always soft and filled with encouragement.

"One step at a time, Ganga," he'd say, his eyes shining with unwavering determination. "We'll get through this together."

Though still frail, Ganga would meet his gaze and nod, her eyes brimming with gratitude. She knew she wouldn't have made it this far without his constant love and support.

Each day brought small but significant victories. First, Ganga could move her fingers, then her arms, and eventually, she took her first steps—with Kewalram's steady hand guiding her. The ordeal they had faced together deepened their bond, strengthening their partnership in ways they had never imagined.

Through every challenge, Kewalram never let go of her hand or his belief in her. His encouragement and dedication became the foundation of Ganga's recovery. Slowly but surely, she began to regain her strength. The road ahead was still long, but they faced it with the certainty that they would walk it together, side by side.

Even as Kewalram devoted himself to Ganga's care, he remained committed to his responsibilities at Oil India. His work remained a priority, but family and close friends stepped in to offer their support and companionship during his absence. The leisurely tennis and bridge games he once enjoyed at the club became a thing of the past, willingly set aside so he could dedicate every available moment to Ganga's recovery.

During this challenging period, Kewalram's strength and devotion stood out—not just as a leader, but as a husband, father, and friend. Balancing his professional responsibilities with the care and love Ganga needed, he became the steadfast pillar of their family. He demonstrated that some battles are not fought in boardrooms or oilfields, but in the quiet moments shared with those we hold dearest.

Amid Ganga's long journey to recovery, a letter arrived that brought unexpected hope. One afternoon, as Kewalram sat by her bedside reading the daily news aloud, a letter bearing a distinct British postage mark was delivered. The envelope, formal and elegant, bore an insignia that caught his attention. As he opened it, his expression shifted to one of amazement.

"It's from Douglas Bader," he said softly, glancing at Ganga with astonishment.

Though still weak, Ganga listened intently. She looked puzzled as Kewalram unfolded the letter and began to read.

Douglas Bader was a legendary Royal Air Force pilot who had become an inspiration worldwide, after losing both legs in a plane crash, continued to serve as a fighter pilot during World War II. His remarkable courage and resilience had made him an icon of determination.

Kewalram began to read the letter aloud:

"Dear Ganga,

I have heard of your strength and determination through friends in India. I wanted to send you a word of encouragement. Fight this battle as I fought mine. The body may falter, but the spirit is boundless. It's not the challenges that define us but how we rise to meet them. Never forget that you have more strength within you than you realize. Believe in it, and you will emerge victorious.

Yours sincerely,

Douglas Bader."

As Kewalram finished, he glanced at Ganga, whose eyes were brimming with tears—not of sorrow, but of renewed hope.

There was more. Along with the letter was a package containing an autographed copy of Bader's book, Reach for the Sky, chronicling his incredible journey of overcoming the impossible. Kewalram handed her the book, the cover embossed with Bader's signature.

"See? Even a hero from across the world believes in you," he said, smiling.

Ganga held the book in her hands, gently tracing her fingers over the cover. Though her body remained frail, something within her shifted that day. If someone like Douglas Bader could find the strength to overcome such immense challenges, then perhaps she could find the courage to do the same.

Meanwhile, in Duliajan, the community's unwavering support remained steadfast. Shri L. Gohain, a master craftsman from the Oil India Workshop, had been quietly working on a special project. Moved by Ganga's condition, he took it upon himself to design custom rehabilitation equipment to aid her recovery. He crafted a sturdy ambulatory crane to help her move around, making it easier for her to stand and walk as she gradually regained her strength.

Kewalram was deeply moved by the thought and effort behind the gesture. When the equipment was brought into their home, Ganga was astonished. Shri Gohain personally explained its functionality, patiently demonstrating how the supports and rails could help her regain balance and mobility. The craftsmanship was impeccable, tailored with care to meet her specific needs. Ganga was overwhelmed by his kindness.

With the aid of the equipment and Kewalram's unwavering encouragement, Ganga began to make steady progress. Each day, Kewalram stood by her side, guiding her through exercises and lifting her spirits whenever frustration arose. His patience and dedication seemed boundless, ensuring she never felt alone in her journey.

"You're doing so well, Ganga," Kewalram would say, gently guiding her hands as she gripped the bars, her legs trembling but resolute in their effort to support her weight. "One step at a time, my love. We'll get there together."

Week by week, Ganga grew stronger. Her once-feeble steps became steadier, and soon she was walking short distances with assistance. This journey became their shared mission—Kewalram devoted his days to helping her with exercises, and in the evenings, they would sit together reading Douglas Bader's book. His inspiring words resonated deeply with them both, turning their nightly reading into a cherished ritual that fueled their determination and strengthened their bond.

Months passed, and one evening, as Ganga stood with the help of the ambulatory crane, she suddenly paused. Kewalram, ever watchful and ready to assist, observed her with quiet concern. Then, something extraordinary happened—Ganga, relying only lightly on the crane for support, took a step forward entirely on her own.

For a moment, silence filled the room. Ganga stood still, her face alight with a mix of disbelief and triumph. She turned to Kewalram, her eyes glistening with emotion.

"I never thought I'd see this day," she whispered, her voice soft yet steady.

Kewalram's eyes filled with tears as he smiled at her. "You're stronger than you realize, Ganga. I always believed you could do it."

As Ganga sat back down, exhausted but proud, Kewalram knelt beside her and gently took her hand gently. "We have so many more years ahead of us," he said, his voice filled with love and quiet determination. "And no matter what comes, we'll face it together—just like this."

Although Ganga's recovery was not yet complete, the hardest part was behind them. Each day brought small but meaningful progress as she steadily regained her independence. The bond between them, already unbreakable, grew even stronger through the challenges they had endured. Together, they had defied the odds, proving that their love and unwavering belief in one another were their greatest sources of strength.

Chapter 15:
Echoes of Legacy

As Kewalram Kanuga's retirement approached, a wave of emotions swept over him, drawing his thoughts into the corridors of memory. Seated in the quiet of their cozy living room, he gazed out of the window, where the evening sky unfolded in hues of warm orange and soft pink. Beside him, his wife, Ganga, offered her steady, reassuring presence. Her knitting needles, once a familiar rhythm in the room, now rested quietly in her lap.

Years ago, Ganga had been forced to abandon her cherished hobby of knitting after a stroke left her left hand and arm immobile. Knitting had been her passion, a way to create cherished gifts for their children and grandchildren. Losing that joy had been a painful adjustment, but Kewalram had never let her feel alone in that struggle.

From that time on, he made it a daily habit to seat her on his right side, gently massaging her left hand and arm while assisting with the therapeutic exercises prescribed by her physiotherapist. It was a quiet, enduring act of love—an unspoken promise to support her, just as she had always supported him.

He leaned back in his chair, memories of his long career at Oil India Limited swirling around him like the gentle breeze outside. As if on instinct, he began guiding Ganga's hand through her therapeutic exercises, his movements gentle and practiced. She watched him with eyes full of affection, her love for him evident in her gaze.

"Do you remember the early days when the Naharkatiya oilfield was first discovered?" Kewalram began, his voice soft and filled with nostalgia.

Ganga looked up, her right hand resting in her lap as he gently held her left. "Of course I do, Kanuga ji," she replied warmly, though her voice had grown a little slower with time.

Kewalram's gaze grew distant as he reminisced. "The mornings there were always crisp, the air rich with the scent of earth and oil. I'd stand by the wells, watching the teams work tirelessly. The hum of the machinery, the clang of tools—it became a melody I cherished. Back then, we were on the brink of something monumental."

Ganga smiled, her knitting now forgotten in her lap, though the passion for their shared journey still shone in her eyes. "I remember how proud you were. You came home with a sparkle in your eyes."

"Yes," Kewalram replied, his smile widening as the memories resurfaced. "The refinery report... I knew we had everything in place. We collected production data from fifteen wells, and that report became the foundation for the Gauhati refinery. It may have seemed like a small victory then, but it was a giant leap for the country."

He leaned forward slightly, the years etched into his face, as he gently massaged Ganga's palm with his fingers. "But it wasn't just about the wells," he said, his voice carrying the weight of experience. "It was about innovation—daring to achieve what others thought was impossible. Do you remember the crude oil conditioning plant? 1963, right there at the site. We separated gas and water from crude oil—a feat many believed was too ambitious."

His wife smiled softly. "I remember how certain you were that it would work."

"It had to," he replied with a knowing smile. "I told the team, 'We need to lead, not follow.' And we did. We pioneered techniques no one had attempted before—gas-based turbines for power generation, deviated drilling, dual-completion wells. We broke new ground, pushed boundaries, and it worked. We maximized efficiency, ensured production stability, and we made a real difference—not just for OIL, but for India's future."

His words lingered in the air, the weight of those accomplishments slowly sinking in. He continued, his voice steady yet reflective, as he gently adjusted her arm to encourage movement. "Back in Duliajan, our office was a buzzing hub of energy."Engineers and geologists from across India came to learn from us. Despite the attention, I always reminded the team that our work wasn't just for OIL—it was for the nation's future. It was for something far bigger than ourselves."

His wife gently squeezed his hand with her right, her eyes glistening with pride. "You always thought about the bigger picture."

Kewalram smiled at her, his movements with her hand growing slower and gentler as the memories played in his mind like an old film reel. "And then there was Kharsang in NEFA—now Arunachal Pradesh. Everyone thought drilling there was too risky, but I saw the potential. Around the same time, we discovered the Kusijan hydrocarbon structure. I remember one of the geologists saying it felt like finding buried treasure."

He laughed softly, shaking his head at the memory. "I told him, 'Treasure for the country.'"

For a moment, the room was still, both of them lost in their thoughts. Then Kewalram spoke again, his voice softer and more contemplative, his fingers continuing their gentle movements over Ganga's arm. "But the pipelines—that was our greatest achievement. The 401-kilometer pipeline from Naharkatiya to Gauhati, completed on March 7, 1962. An engineering marvel, cutting through dense jungles, crossing rivers, and winding over hills. And just a month later, on April 26, we started pumping crude oil to the Gauhati refinery. People doubted we'd meet the deadline, but we did."

He shook his head slowly, still in awe of the achievement. "And we didn't stop there. In 1963, we completed another pipeline—757 kilometers long—stretching from Naharkatiya to Barauni. On June 30, 1964, the first oil flowed to the Barauni refinery. That wasn't just infrastructure; it was the lifeblood of India's growth and development."

He looked at Ganga, his eyes softening with emotion. "Those pipelines weren't just steel tubes. They were our vision—connecting Assam's oil fields to the rest of the country, fueling progress, and sparking industrial growth."

The sun had slipped below the horizon, casting the room in a warm, dusky glow. Kewalram's voice grew quieter, more introspective. "I remember one evening, standing by the crude oil conditioning plant, watching the sun set over the fields. A junior engineer approached me, his voice filled with awe. He said, 'It's amazing, sir. We've really come a long way.'"

Kewalram smiled softly at the memory. "I looked at him and said, 'Yes, we have. But there's still more to do.'"

His wife's reassuring smile met his gaze. "You've done so much. Your legacy will always be a part of OIL."

He nodded, the years weighing on his shoulders yet a quiet lightness settling in his heart as he gently placed Ganga's hand back in her lap. "Yes," he said softly, "I suppose it will."

In the twilight of his career, Kewalram Kanuga sat there, comforted by the knowledge that the work to which he had dedicated his life would endure, shaping the nation's future long after he was gone. But above all, it was these quiet moments with Ganga—massaging her hand and reliving their shared memories—that reminded him of the love that had carried them through it all.

Chapter 16:
The Early Retirement

By 1969, Duliajan had transformed into a thriving township in every sense. Kanuga, now approaching the end of his career at Oil India, had witnessed this remarkable journey firsthand. He had seen Duliajan evolve from a mere set of blueprints and a vision into a vibrant community teeming with life and opportunity. Many who had once hesitated to leave Digboi now proudly called Duliajan their home, embracing the town as a symbol of progress and belonging.

Despite his impending retirement, Kanuga remained deeply committed to the town's daily life. He continued to visit the school, the clubs, and the oil fields, offering his unwavering guidance and support. To the residents of Duliajan, Kanuga was more than a leader—he was a family.

Duliajan—Kewalram's life's work—had flourished beyond recognition. What was once barren land had transformed into a bustling township, a living testament to his vision and unwavering dedication. Oil India had risen to prominence as a key player in the nation's energy sector, with Duliajan at its core. Yet, for Kanuga, his proudest achievement wasn't the company's success. It was the vibrant, close-knit community he had nurtured—a town alive with families, schools, clubs, and an enduring sense of belonging. Under his guidance, Duliajan had become much more than a workplace; it had become a home.

In November 1969, Kewalram Kanuga faced a pivotal moment in his life. At 56, after decades of devoted service to Oil India Limited, he made the difficult decision to retire early—18 months before reaching the official retirement age of 58. It was not a choice made lightly.

Kanuga had been a cornerstone of the company, guiding its growth with vision and dedication.

However, times were changing. The departure of Managing Director John Campbell Finlay to the UK left a leadership void. While Kanuga's experience and accomplishments made him the obvious candidate for the top position, government regulations concerning his proximity to retirement age rendered him ineligible. At the time, Kanuga was serving as Resident Director at Oil India's Field Headquarters in Duliajan—a role that had grown alongside the thriving township he had helped build.

One afternoon, as Kanuga sat reviewing plans for the final phase of Duliajan's housing and infrastructure expansion, a knock on his office door broke his concentration.

"KB, you've done it again!" exclaimed Mr. K. C. Roy, his trusted colleague and successor as Resident Chief Executive after Kanuga's impending retirement. Roy entered the room with a broad grin. "The board just approved the final phase of the township expansion. You've secured Duliajan's future."

Kanuga smiled warmly, though his eyes carried a hint of sadness. "It's been quite a journey, Roy. Hard to believe that just over a decade ago, this place was nothing more than a blueprint."

"And now it's a thriving town," Roy replied, settling into the chair across from him. "All thanks to you. So, what's next, KB? Have you thought about it much?"

Kanuga nodded, though the weight of the decision was evident. "Retirement is just around the corner. But stepping away from something that's been your life's work... it's not easy."

Roy, sensing the inner conflict in Kanuga's words, leaned forward, his tone serious. "KB, I've heard you're thinking about leaving earlier than planned. Are you sure this is the right decision? Eighteen more months—that's all. With a little more time, you could take Oil India to even greater heights. The company needs you. We all do."

Kanuga sighed, his expression softening with thought. "Roy, this decision hasn't come easily. I've wrestled with it for months. But the truth is, the company is evolving, and while I've built a lot here, it's time for someone else to lead. Oil India is bigger than any one person, and I know it will continue to thrive without me. I'm ready to embrace a new chapter in my life."

Roy shook his head gently, his admiration for Kanuga unmistakable. "You're the heart and soul of this place, KB. To you, Oil India isn't just a company—it's a community. That's why I'm asking you to reconsider. You've always put the people first, and that's what makes you irreplaceable."

Kanuga smiled at his friend, his expression a mix of gratitude and finality. "Thank you, Roy. That means a lot. But this isn't about walking away from responsibility—it's about recognizing the right time to pass the torch. Duliajan and its people will be fine. I've laid the foundation for the future, and I trust it's in capable hands now."

Roy exhaled deeply, realizing Kanuga's decision was final. "You didn't just build this town, KB—you built its future. That's something no one will ever forget."

Kanuga's eyes shimmered with emotion as he rose and extended his hand. "Thank you, Roy. That means more to me than you know. While I may be leaving, a part of me will always remain here in Duliajan."

As Kanuga gazed out the window at the thriving township he had nurtured, a wave of bittersweet pride washed over him. The choice to retire had not been easy, but he knew it was the right one. Duliajan would continue to grow and thrive, its foundations forever bearing the quiet legacy of the man who had helped build it from the ground up.

As news of Kanuga's retirement spread, the township began preparing for his departure. Everywhere he went, people shared quiet words of appreciation, stories of his kindness and vision, and heartfelt gestures of gratitude. Workers, shopkeepers, and families alike held him in the highest regard.

One afternoon, as Kanuga strolled through the OIL Market, a familiar voice called out, "Kanuga Sahab!"

A shopkeeper greeted him with a broad smile. "We've heard you're retiring soon. It won't be the same without you."

Kanuga returned the smile and shook his head gently. "The township will do just fine. I may be stepping away, but Duliajan has its own strength now."

Another worker stepped forward, extending his hand. "You've done so much for us, sahab. We'll never forget it. Our children are growing up in a place they're proud to call home."

Those words lingered in Kanuga's mind. His dream had never been just to build an industrial hub; he had envisioned Duliajan as a place where families could grow, thrive, and take pride in their community. Now, standing among the very people he had worked so hard for, he knew that dream had become a reality.

Later that evening, as Kewalram sat on the porch with Ganga, watching the township lights flicker in the distance, a quiet contentment settled over him.

"We've built something lasting here," he said softly.

Ganga, always his unwavering support, smiled warmly. "You've built more than a township. You've built a community—a home for generations to come."

As they sat together under the evening sky, watching Duliajan bathed in its serene glow, Kewalram Kanuga felt a deep sense of peace. His legacy was not confined to the oil fields or the infrastructure he had helped build; it lived on in the hearts and lives of the people who proudly called Duliajan their home.

As they sat together under the evening sky, watching Duliajan bathed in its serene glow, Kewalram Kanuga felt a deep sense of peace. His legacy was not confined to the oil fields or the infrastructure he had helped build; it lived on in the hearts and lives of the people who proudly called Duliajan their home.

As his retirement approached, the Oil India Higher Secondary School organized a special event to honor him. Since its inception, the school had thrived, becoming a cornerstone of the community. On this momentous day, the campus buzzed with life—students, teachers, and parents gathered, their lives touched by the educational opportunities Kanuga had so passionately championed.

Standing by his side was his son, Lakshman, now a confident young man in his twenties, beaming with pride. Together, they listened as the headmaster, Mr. Hare Krishna Das, addressed the gathering, paying tribute to Kanuga's remarkable contributions.

"Kanuga Sir's vision has transformed the lives of every student who has walked these halls," Mr. Das said, his voice thick with emotion. "Because of his unwavering dedication, our children have the chance to excel, to dream, and to achieve. For this, we are eternally grateful."

The crowd erupted into heartfelt applause as Kanuga rose from his seat, his eyes scanning the sea of young, eager faces before him. Memories flooded back—his own children had once sat in these very classrooms. Now, seeing the next generation filled his heart with pride and hope.

"Education," Kanuga began, his voice steady and warm, "is the foundation of progress. Through education, we build our future, and here, in this school, I see the future of Duliajan."

He paused, his gaze lingering on the children in the audience. "It has been my greatest honor to walk this journey alongside all of you. As I prepare to step down from my role at Oil India, I do so with confidence, knowing that this township—this community—is in capable hands.

The work we have done together will endure, and I am certain that Duliajan's brightest days are yet to come."

The applause was thunderous, yet amid the cheers, Kewalram Kanuga stood quietly, a profound sense of fulfillment settling over him. He was surrounded by the very people whose lives he had touched, their gratitude reflecting the impact of his work.

At the helm of Oil India during this period was Mr. Devakanta Barooah, the renowned poet and politician from Assam. Barooah was more than a leader; he was a visionary who deeply understood Assam's cultural and social fabric and its inseparable connection to Oil India. He held immense respect for Kanuga, the man who had overseen Duliajan's transformation and played a pivotal role in shaping Oil India into a thriving organization.

In the week leading up to Kanuga's retirement, Duliajan's clubs and organizations came together to honor him with a series of heartfelt events. The Zaloni Club hosted a memorable farewell evening, complete with a spirited tennis match, a sumptuous dinner, and vibrant cultural performances. Meanwhile, the Duliajan Club organized an exhilarating football match, followed by a joyous celebration that brought the entire community together.

At a farewell gathering at the Duliajan Club, Mr. Devakanta Barooah, the chairman, took the podium with his characteristic eloquence. Known for his poetic brilliance, his words carried the weight of admiration and gratitude as he spoke about Kanuga's enduring legacy.

"Kewalram Kanuga," Barooah began, his voice steady yet laced with emotion, "is not just a name tied to the early days of Oil India. He is a symbol of perseverance, vision, and integrity. He has shaped this company as a sculptor shapes his masterpiece—with patience, precision, and care. And, just as a sculptor's work stands the test of time, so too will Kanuga's contributions be remembered for generations."

The audience—officers and workers alike—listened intently, their faces reflecting pride and respect. Kanuga had been more than an officer; he was a guiding light, a leader who placed the well-being of every individual associated with the company at the heart of his work.

Barooah continued, "It is rare to find a man whose work unites everyone—officers and workers alike. Today, as we bid farewell, we are not just saying goodbye to a colleague or a leader. We are bidding farewell to the man who has shaped Oil India into what it is today."

The audience responded with a resounding applause, not the perfunctory kind often heard at formal gatherings, but a genuine expression of admiration and a touch of sadness as the reality of Kanuga's departure began to sink in.

Kanuga, ever humble despite his remarkable achievements, stood quietly, absorbing the moment. For him, it was never about the accolades or the grandeur of the ceremonies. What truly mattered were the heartfelt gestures, like the farewells organized by the labor union and the sweeper union. These simple yet profound events meant more to him than any official recognition—they validated the values he had upheld throughout his career: respect for every individual, regardless of their rank or role.

In his brief yet heartfelt response, Kanuga spoke with his trademark humility, expressing gratitude to everyone who had worked alongside him over the years. "Oil India is not the work of one man," he said. "It is the result of the collective effort of each and every person here. I was merely one among you, fortunate to be in a position to help guide us forward. The true strength of this company lies in its people."

It was a fitting conclusion to a career defined not only by outstanding professional achievements but also by Kanuga's unique ability to unite people—across departments, roles, and social divides. He had always believed that a company's true greatness lay not in its infrastructure or profits but in the dedication and spirit of the people who worked tirelessly every day to make it thrive.

As the farewell ceremonies came to an end, the township was filled with a profound sense of loss. With Kanuga's departure, it felt as though something truly irreplaceable was slipping away. His retirement marked not just the end of an era but the conclusion of a chapter crafted with care, wisdom, and a profound respect for everyone who had played a role in Oil India's success.

One evening, as Kewalram and Ganga sat together watching the festivities unfold, Ganga turned to her husband with a warm smile. "You've touched so many lives here," she said softly. "This community owes much of what it is to you."

Kewalram, ever the humble soul, smiled and shook his head. "It wasn't just me, Ganga," he said gently. "The people of Duliajan built this town as much as I did."

Ganga nodded, her eyes reflecting the admiration she felt for her husband. His humility was one of the many qualities that endeared him to everyone. "But you showed them the way," she replied. "And they'll carry that forward."

Kewalram felt a deep sense of peace in her words. His journey in Duliajan had been long, filled with challenges, and immensely rewarding. As he prepared to embrace the next chapter of his life, he knew his legacy would endure—etched into the township, the lives of its people, and the future they would continue to build together.

Kewalram Kanuga's early retirement brought its own challenges. His retirement home in New Delhi was still under construction and would take another two years to be completed. For someone accustomed to the structured life at Oil India, where every challenge was tackled head-on, this period of waiting felt unusually unsettling. Yet, as so often in his life, fate presented him with a new opportunity.

During this transitional phase, Kanuga was approached by India Carbon, a company seeking seasoned leadership for a new venture. They offered him the role of President of Special Projects, tasking him with establishing a calcined petroleum coke project in Goa. The proposal wasn't just a professional challenge—it resonated deeply on a personal level.

Kanuga had long envisioned creating communities like Duliajan, where industrial work coexisted with a self-sufficient, nurturing environment for residents. This project in Goa felt like a natural extension of that dream, giving him an opportunity to build something meaningful once again.

One evening, as Ganga sat with Kewalram on the veranda of their temporary home in Calcutta, sipping tea, she spoke with quiet resolve. Despite the challenges of her recovery after a stroke, her voice remained steady. "Goa will be different," she said thoughtfully.

Kewalram smiled warmly. "It'll give us a breather. By the time the project is completed, the house in Delhi will be ready. And for you, it'll mean a refreshing change of scenery."

Ganga returned his smile. "A change of scenery does sound nice. But are you sure you want to jump into another big project so soon after retiring?"

Leaning back in his chair, he looked at her with a familiar determination. "You know me, Ganga. I can't sit idle. There's work to be done, and I've always loved it—whether it's building townships or nurturing communities."

Kanuga accepted the role but chose not to relocate to Goa. Instead, he managed operations from Calcutta, collaborating closely with the American technology partner, The Great Lakes Corporation, based in the USA. His work required frequent travel between Calcutta and Goa, where he oversaw negotiations, finalized the project site, and navigated complex land transfer discussions with the influential Dempo Group, a dominant force in Goa's business landscape.

True to his nature, Kanuga approached the task with unwavering dedication. From his base in Calcutta, he coordinated meetings, worked with engineers, and negotiated with precision, drawing on his years of experience. Every few weeks, he flew to Goa, spending days immersed in land acquisition talks, technical planning, and site development. During these trips, he carefully selected the plant's location, envisioning not just the industrial infrastructure but also the homes, schools, and community spaces that could eventually grow around it—a vision rooted in his commitment to building holistic, self-sufficient communities.

The early months of the Goa project were marked by excitement and promise. Kewalram Kanuga tackled the new venture with the same energy and determination that had defined his career. Establishing a calcined petroleum coke plant was a formidable challenge, but Kanuga was no stranger to ambitious undertakings.

Plans were meticulously crafted, and within weeks, he had built a skilled team of engineers, architects, and project managers. Together, they worked tirelessly, turning concepts into reality. Blueprints lined the walls of his office, and each meeting buzzed with discussions about progress, challenges, and possibilities. The sense of purpose was palpable, driving the team forward with unwavering focus.

One evening, after a long day of negotiations with the Dempo Group, Kanuga called Ganga from his hotel in Goa. "We're making progress," he said, his voice filled with excitement. "It's coming together. The land deal looks promising."

On the other end, Ganga's voice was calm yet encouraging. "That's good to hear," she said. "Just don't overwork yourself with all this traveling."

Kanuga smiled, knowing she couldn't see it. "You know me. I thrive on this. It feels like Duliajan all over again—a chance to build something from scratch."

This was Kanuga's element—overseeing every detail, from the design of the plant to the selection of equipment, while imagining the broader community he aspired to create. For him, the project wasn't just about industrial production; it was about building a self-sustaining township where workers could live comfortably, families could thrive, and the local economy could flourish.

The parallels to his early days in Duliajan were unmistakable, and that memory became his driving force. Over evening tea, he often shared his thoughts with Ganga, his eyes lighting up as he spoke about the possibilities. The vision of creating something meaningful once again filled him with a renewed sense of purpose.

One evening, as the sun set over the Arabian Sea, Kanuga stood with his team at the project site, surveying the progress. The first foundations had been laid, and a sense of accomplishment filled the air. "We're on our way," he said, turning to Mr. D'Silva, the India Carbon manager who had become his trusted ally on the ground.

D'Silva, known for his calm demeanor and sharp insights, nodded with a smile. "The team's putting in great effort. If all goes as planned, we'll have this plant operational within two years. Goa is the perfect place for this."

Kanuga returned the smile, pride welling up in him—the same pride he had felt when the first structures of Duliajan began to take shape. It felt as though everything was coming together. Goa had embraced him, and the project's future looked bright, filled with promise and possibility.

But, as is often the case in life, events took an unforeseen turn.

One afternoon, a seemingly routine letter from the Ministry of Industry arrived at Kanuga's office. He was reviewing the day's reports when his secretary handed him the envelope. At first glance, it appeared to be just another standard update. However, as Kanuga read through the document, his expression grew tense.

The letter outlined a sudden policy change by the government, driven by shifts in global markets and mounting economic pressures. The new regulations aimed to restrict aluminium exports, prioritizing domestic consumption instead. This decision directly threatened the calcined petroleum coke project, which was designed to produce a critical ingredient for aluminium production. With the government scaling back on aluminium, the plant's future demand—and viability—was now in serious doubt.

Kanuga quickly assembled his core team for an urgent meeting. In the conference room, a tense silence settled over the group as they absorbed the gravity of the policy change.

Breaking the silence, Mr. D'Silva spoke in a measured but grave tone. "This is a serious setback. Without the aluminium market, there's no demand for our product. We're facing a challenging situation."Kanuga nodded, his thoughts racing. "We've already invested so much. Abandoning the project now would be disastrous, but moving forward without a clear market isn't viable either."

For days, he and his team explored every possible alternative. They met with government officials, hoping for an exemption or a policy revision, and even considered redirecting the project to serve other industries. Yet, every option seemed increasingly unfeasible. The plant was purpose-built for aluminium production, and reconfiguring it at this stage would demand both time and funds they no longer had.

After a grueling week of meetings and dead ends, Kanuga returned to Calcutta—disheartened but not defeated. In the days that followed, the inevitable decision was made: the calcined petroleum coke project would be abandoned. Months of planning, negotiations, and relentless effort were set aside, undone by circumstances beyond their control.

As always, Ganga was a pillar of support. That evening, when Kanuga returned home weary and disheartened, she joined him on the veranda, quietly listening as he recounted the events.

"I'm sorry," she said gently, placing her hand over his. "I know how much this project meant to you."

Kanuga sighed, leaning back in his chair. "It's hard to let go, especially when we were so close. But sometimes, there's just no way forward."

"Sometimes," Ganga agreed, her voice was calm but resolute. "But you've always found a way to move on."

And she was right. Though the setback was significant, it was not the end of Kanuga's career. Recognizing his skills and leadership, India Carbon soon transferred him to their operations in Delhi, appointing him as Liaison Chief. In this new role, he took on the challenge of managing a diversification portfolio, applying his expertise to a wider range of industries and opening the door to fresh opportunities.

The Goa project became one of the rare instances in Kanuga's life where, despite meticulous planning and relentless effort, success slipped through his fingers. Yet, as he and Ganga prepared to leave for Delhi, he carried with him the understanding that every challenge—whether realized or abandoned—was a step in the larger journey. Resilient as ever, Kanuga knew this was just one chapter, and his story was far from over.

In the months that followed, Kewalram adjusted to life in Delhi. Though the Goa venture had been brief, it served as a transitional phase, allowing him to refocus and look ahead. By the early 1970s, when their new home in New Delhi was ready, Kewalram Kanuga retired from India Carbon, marking the start of a new chapter for him and Ganga.

As he settled into the quiet rhythm of post-retirement life, Kewalram often reflected on his remarkable journey. From his humble beginnings as a junior clerical assistant in a British company, to mastering field operations, becoming the first Indian General Manager of Oil India, and eventually serving as a Director on its inaugural board, his career had been a tapestry of milestones—some celebrated publicly, others deeply personal.

The Goa project, though incomplete, was just another chapter in a life defined by resilience, progress, and purpose. For Kewalram, success was never about a single achievement but about the legacy of growth and perseverance he left behind.

Chapter 17:
The Kanuga Legacy Continues

As K.B. Kanuga's professional career thrived, his personal life was equally rich and fulfilling. A trailblazer in the oil industry, he was also a devoted family man, blessed with six children—three sons and three daughters. Each of them embraced the values of dedication, hard work, and education that he had instilled in them from an early age.

His eldest daughter, Mira, held a special place in his heart. A brilliant student, she graduated from Cotton College, Gauhati, and went on to pursue her postgraduate studies at the prestigious London School of Economics. Kanuga deeply admired her intelligence and independence and took great pride in seeing her forge her own path in life.

Mira married Hiroo Khushalani, an engineer working with AOC, and the couple built a loving home in New Delhi, where they raised their children, Vivek and Raksha. Now in their later years, Mira and Hiroo continue to embody the grace and resilience that have defined their lives, cherishing the love and bonds of their close-knit family.

Kaushalya, Kewalram's second daughter, inherited her father's strong sense of responsibility and dedication to the community. After completing her undergraduate studies at Cotton College in Gauhati and her postgraduate education at Presidency College in Kolkata, she returned to Duliajan to work as a teacher at Oil India Higher Secondary School. During her college years, Kaushalya served as the debating secretary at Cotton College, a role that highlighted her intellect and leadership abilities.

Later, she moved to Kolkata after marrying Ganesh Prasad Singh, where they built a life together. Following her husband's untimely passing, Kaushalya remained a steadfast pillar for her family, raising her children, Saurabh and Snigdha, with unwavering strength and grace. Saurabh took charge of the family business, successfully expanding its operations in surgical cotton and medical accessories. Meanwhile, Snigdha pursued a career in London, eventually becoming a divisional director at American Express.

Kanuga's eldest son, Nandlal, shared his father's talent for numbers. After graduating from St.Edmond's in Shillong, he pursued a career as a Chartered Accountant, completing his training in Scotland. His untimely passing was a profound loss to the family, but Kewalram found solace in the legacy Nandlal left behind.

Nandlal's wife, Veena, continued to live in Bengaluru, nurturing their family. Their children, Avinash and Mamta, carried forward his legacy in their own ways. Avinash built a successful career as a banker, while Mamta dedicated herself to homemaking and raising her family. Kewalram often reflected on Nandlal's life with a mix of pride and sorrow, cherishing the lasting impact his son had made in his brief but meaningful time.

Girdharilal, Kewalram's second son, chose a path entirely different from his siblings, venturing into the field of medicine. He earned his MBBS degree from Assam Medical College, Dibrugarh, and later specialized in obstetrics and gynecology in London, where he became an MRCOG.

Now settled in London with his wife, Beena, Girdharilal's family has endured their share of heartache, particularly with the loss of their daughter, Komal. Despite this tragedy, their son, Puneet, has flourished as a successful hotelier. Kewalram drew comfort from Girdharilal's resilience, recognizing in his son the same steadfast spirit he had always tried to embody.

Leelawanti, the fifth of Kewalram's children, inherited her father's discipline and keen eye for detail. After graduating from Cotton College, she pursued a diploma in housekeeping at Nirmala Niketan in Mumbai.

Leelawanti built a successful career in the garment export industry, dedicating many years to her work before retiring from a multinational corporation. Now settled in New Delhi, she enjoys a quieter life, though her industrious spirit and unwavering dedication remain key aspects of her identity.

Lakshman, the youngest of the Kanuga children, was perhaps the one who most closely mirrored his father's ambition and intellect. He began his academic journey as part of the first batch of Higher Secondary School in Duliajan, followed by undergraduate studies at Cotton College, Gauhati.

Lakshman's pursuit of excellence led him to earn a postgraduate certificate in International Marketing from the London School of Management and a PhD in Corporate Management from the EU University in Paris. Now residing in Gurgaon with his daughter, Upasana, Lakshman has built a remarkable career in corporate management. He remains a living embodiment of the values his father held dear: education, hard work, and an unwavering commitment to excellence.

As K.B. Kanuga reflected on his life, his pride extended beyond his contributions to Oil India Limited and the development of Duliajan. It was the accomplishments of his children that truly brought him joy. Each of them, in their unique way, had carried forward the values that had shaped his own life.

Whether in medicine, corporate management, family businesses, or multinational corporations, the Kanuga children had built remarkable legacies of their own. Their achievements were firmly rooted in the principles their father had instilled: education, perseverance, and a deep commitment to the community.

Though scattered across India and the world, the Kanuga family remained closely connected, united by the values and love of K.B. Kanuga and his wife, Ganga, had nurtured in their home. During family reunions, as they shared stories of their lives and achievements, there was always a sense of continuity—a shared understanding that their father's legacy was far more than oil wells and pipelines.

It was a legacy of family, education, and the unwavering belief that hard work and dedication could make anything possible. In the end, K.B. Kanuga's greatest contribution was not just his professional accomplishments but the enduring legacy of integrity and achievement he left behind—a legacy that would continue to inspire his children and their descendants for generations.

Chapter 18:
Life After Retirement

A year after retiring from the dynamic world of oil and gas, Kewalram Kanuga felt a growing sense of restlessness.

While retirement offered a slower pace, his sharp mind remained active, seeking meaningful ways to give back to the community he had helped shape over decades. One quiet afternoon, while he and Ganga enjoyed the serene atmosphere of their New Delhi home, a new idea started to take shape.

"I've been thinking," Kewalram said, breaking the stillness on the veranda. "There are so many of us—'old boys,' as we called ourselves—who worked in the oil fields of Assam. Many might need help now, whether it's camaraderie or a sense of belonging."

Ganga glanced up from her book, curiosity lighting her eyes. "And what are you planning this time?" she asked with a knowing smile.

"A trust, a fellowship," Kewalram said thoughtfully. "To support the old boys—not just financially, but emotionally too. Many don't have pensions that cover the rising costs of healthcare, and they miss the companionship of their former colleagues."

His mind buzzed with possibilities as he quickly drafted a letter to the Burmah Oil headquarters in London. In it, he outlined his vision for the "Old Boys Association" (OBA), an initiative aimed at fostering fellowship among retired oil workers from Assam Oil in Digboi and Oil India in Duliajan, while also providing financial support to those in need.

Weeks went by as Kewalram kept himself occupied with small tasks, though his mind often drifted back to the letter he had sent. One morning, an envelope arrived bearing the official seal of Burmah Oil.

With growing anticipation, he opened it and read the response from Sir Alaister Downe, the chairman of the board. It wasn't merely a polite acknowledgment—it was a wholehearted endorsement of his plan. Burmah Oil had approved a £10,000 grant to establish the Old Boys Association.

"It's happening," Kewalram said to Ganga that evening, his voice filled with quiet satisfaction. "The trust is becoming a reality."

Ganga's eyes sparkled with pride. "You've always had a gift for bringing people together," she said warmly.

Establishing the Old Boys Association required meticulous planning, particularly in setting up and managing the Burmah Oil Pensioners' Trust (BOPT), which would oversee the funds. Kewalram knew that assembling the right team was crucial, and two individuals stood out for their invaluable contributions.

"Vasudevan has been indispensable in this process," Kewalram remarked to Ganga one day, almost as if speaking to himself.

K. Vasudevan, the Chief Internal Auditor at Assam Oil in Digboi, had taken the lead in structuring the trust and overseeing its operations. He had meticulously compiled a list of pensioners from both Assam Oil Company (AOC) and Oil India, laying the groundwork for the membership drive that would help the Old Boys Association thrive.

"His expertise in financial matters has been invaluable," Kewalram said, his appreciation unmistakable. "Without his attention to detail, we wouldn't have the solid foundation we do now. It's one thing to have a vision, but executing it with such precision is entirely another."

But Vasudevan was only part of the equation. Equally important was C.R. Jagannathan, whose efforts were pivotal in securing the financial future of the OBA.

"Jags, now there's a man who knows how to get things done," Kewalram remarked with admiration.

With his strong connections to Burmah Castrol, Jagannathan had gone above and beyond to bolster the trust's financial foundation. While Burmah Oil had initially pledged £10,000 to the corpus, Jagannathan's determination secured an additional £10,000 from Burmah Castrol, effectively doubling the trust's funds.

Kewalram vividly recalled the moment Jagannathan shared the news. "Jags walked in with a smile, and I immediately knew he'd accomplished something significant. He doubled the corpus—£20,000 instead of £10,000. It was a complete game-changer."

With Vasudevan and Jagannathan by his side, Kewalram had built the foundation for something that would endure well beyond his time at Oil India. The Old Boys Association wasn't just an act of goodwill; it was a vital lifeline for those who had dedicated their careers to the company and now needed support in their retirement years.

As the trust's formalities were finalized, Kewalram felt a deep sense of gratitude for the team that had brought his vision to life. The Old Boys Association was more than just financial assistance—it was a way to honour and support the people who had been the heart and soul of Oil India and Assam Oil. For Kewalram, who had always believed in the power of building communities, the OBA was a true reflection of that belief.

The Old Boys Association quickly became an integral part of the Oil India community. It wasn't just about the legacy of oil wells and pipelines—it was about the people and the enduring bonds they had built over the years. For Kewalram, this was his greatest achievement. The OBA ensured that no one would be forgotten, no matter how much time passed.

With the funds secured, Kewalram wasted no time in formalizing the association. A modest joining fee of Rs 300 was set, making membership accessible to nearly all pensioners. Word spread rapidly through the oil community, and soon, old friends and colleagues were eagerly signing up, thrilled at the chance to reconnect.

A few months later, the inaugural meeting of the OBA took place in Duliajan, a fitting venue at the heart of their shared careers. As Kewalram stepped into the room filled with familiar faces, a wave of warmth washed over him. Men who had once worked alongside him in the oil fields greeted him with hearty handshakes and embraces, their spouses standing proudly by their sides.

"It feels just like old times," said B M Chopra, a longtime colleague from the Digboi days, giving Kewalram a friendly pat on the back.

Kewalram grinned. "Exactly like old times."

The OBA quickly became a beloved part of life for retired oil workers. Each year, they gathered to reminisce, share stories, and offer mutual support. The trust, funded by interest from the corpus, provided financial assistance for medical emergencies and, in some cases, even for basic needs like food and housing.

As time passed, the OBA also took on the role of advocating for pension reform. The old boys, left behind by shifting economic landscapes, campaigned for inflation indexing and other adjustments to ensure retirees could live with dignity.

"Do you think they'll listen to us, Kanuga ji?" Ganga asked one evening as Kewalram worked on a petition to the government.

"They'll have to," he replied firmly. "We built this industry. We deserve dignity in retirement."

Over the years, the OBA grew not just in numbers but in purpose. It became a family, united by the shared hardships and triumphs of life in the oil fields. At its heart was Kewalram Kanuga, still bringing people together and building something meaningful, even in retirement.

At one of the annual meetings, as he surveyed the room filled with smiling faces, Kewalram felt a profound sense of fulfillment. His career had spanned decades, but the legacy of the Old Boys Association—the rekindled friendships, the support offered—was something that would endure long after the last drop of oil was extracted from the fields of Digboi and Duliajan.

After settling into their new home in Delhi, KB Kanuga discovered that retirement suited him far more than he had anticipated. The days were peaceful, filled with quiet reflection, cherished moments with Ganga, and occasional visits from their now-grown children, each busy with their own lives. Yet, even in the stillness of this new chapter, Kanuga's thoughts often drifted back to Assam—to Duliajan, the oil fields, and the colleagues with whom he had spent countless years building something truly meaningful.

One evening, as the sun dipped below the horizon, Kewalram sat on the porch, lost in thought. Ganga joined him, a steaming cup of tea in hand. "Thinking about Assam again, aren't you?" she asked, her knowing smile breaking the silence.

Kewalram returned the smile. "It's hard not to. So much of who I am was shaped there."

He leaned back in his chair, the memories of Duliajan flooding back. As General Manager of Oil India Limited, he had witnessed the oil fields of Naharkatiya and Moran thrive under his leadership. What had once been scattered wells in Assam's remote corners had grown into one of India's most productive oil operations.

"You know, Ganga," he began quietly, his voice tinged with nostalgia, "it wasn't just about drilling for oil. It was about something bigger. We were pioneers."

Ganga looked up from her book, her eyes warm with affection. "You always did have that vision," she said softly, her smile reflecting his pride.

He smiled softly, the sound more a memory than a laugh. "I still remember when we commissioned the world's first crude oil conditioning plant back in '63. It was such a proud day—not just for me, but for the entire team. We introduced techniques like deviated drilling and dual completion that no one had ever attempted before."

He paused, his voice softening as his thoughts shifted. "But it wasn't just the work," he added, almost to himself. "It was the people."

Ganga glanced at him with a knowing smile, her cup of tea cradled in her hands. "You always cared more about the people than the work. That's what made you different."

His mind wandered back to Duliajan, the place where they had spent so much of their lives. "Do you remember when we first arrived there? It was nothing but jungle and tea estates. But we built something from it. Roads, houses, schools... and the hospital."

He leaned forward slightly, his tone earnest. "I made sure that hospital became one of the best in the region—not just for the officers, but for the workers too. That little dispensary grew into the Oil India Hospital because I knew it had to be more than just a workplace. It had to be a community."

"You've always had a heart for the people," Ganga said softly, her voice warm with admiration.

A fond smile spread across his face. "Do you remember Bruno Banerjee?"

Ganga's eyes lit up with recognition. "Of course I do! The man from Calcutta—so full of energy. How could I forget?"

Kanuga nodded. "Yes, that's him. His son, Victor, went on to become a famous actor. But Bruno—he was something else. A force of nature. Always Passionate and deeply caring. I'll never forget the day he came to me in the late sixties with an idea. He wanted to start a school for visually impaired children. It wasn't just charity for him; it was personal."

"And you helped him," Ganga said, her voice tinged with pride.

"I had to," Kanuga replied. "He wasn't asking for money; he was asking for belief. And I believed in him. Oil India backed the project, and it wasn't just about funding—we championed it. It became something we all cared deeply about."

"You always did support causes that mattered," Ganga said with a smile.

Kanuga leaned forward slightly, his hands resting on his knees. "Bruno and I shared more than just that project. We both had a passion for sports. He played alongside legends like Dhyan Chand in hockey and Sailen Manna in football. I admired him for that. It made our connection even stronger."

"You respected him, didn't you?" Ganga asked, her voice thoughtful.

Kanuga nodded. "When the new football field in Duliajan was ready, there was no question in my mind—Bruno had to inaugurate it. It wasn't about cutting a ribbon; it was about honouring someone who had given so much to the community."

"And he accepted?" Ganga asked.

Kanuga smiled warmly. "He did. It was a beautiful day. The inauguration wasn't just a ceremony; it was a tribute to everything Bruno represented—teamwork, leadership, and giving back."

They sat in quiet reflection for a moment before Ganga broke the silence. "And the school? What happened to it?"

"It flourished," Kanuga said, his face glowing with pride. "The Moran Blind School became a beacon of hope. The Ladies Club of Duliajan played a pivotal role, raising funds and volunteering tirelessly. To this day, the school thrives. It's a testament to what Bruno and I believed in—that true progress isn't just about industry; it's about uplifting lives."

Ganga looked at him with deep admiration. Much of the school's story was new to her since she had stepped back from the Ladies Club activities during her health struggles. She reached out, gently placing her hand over his, her eyes soft with gratitude. "You've done well, Kanuga ji. You've been more than just an engineer or a leader. You've been someone who truly cared about people."

Kewalram leaned back, exhaling a quiet sigh, his gaze distant and thoughtful. "That's what mattered most, Ganga. The oil, the fields—they were important, of course. But it's the lives we touched, the community we built. That's what I'll cherish the most."

Ganga squeezed his hand gently, her voice tender. "And that's what others will remember too, Kanuga ji. That's your true legacy."

As the evening sun dipped lower, casting a warm golden glow across the room, they sat together in peaceful silence, content in the knowledge that their journey had been one of purpose and connection—a legacy that would continue to shine in the lives they had touched.

Kewalram Kanuga spent most of his retirement years in his modest yet comfortable New Delhi home. It was a place where the warmth of family filled the air, enriched by lively conversations, laughter, and the comings and goings of loved ones. His youngest daughter, Leela, shared the home with him for many years while working at a garment export company in the city. Meanwhile, his eldest daughter, Mira, lived nearby with her family. Their frequent visits brought the house to life, brimming with the energy of children and grandchildren.

In the early years of Kewalram Kanuga's retirement, his home was bustling with life. His second son, Girdhari, lived with him for about three years along with his wife and two young children before the family eventually migrated to the UK. Their presence brought a comforting rhythm to his daily life. Other relatives, including siblings, nieces, and nephews, visited frequently, often bringing food, stories, and a sense of togetherness that made the house feel vibrant. Those were busy days for Kewalram, and the lively commotion of family life filled his heart with joy and lightness.

Yet, a quiet emptiness always lingered beside him. Kewalram's wife, Ganga, had passed away on 6th July 1985, about sixteen years after his retirement, leaving a void that time could not fill.

Kewalram's life was deeply intertwined with that of his wife, Ganga, a woman of simple yet profound values. Her faith and unwavering support formed the cornerstone of their enduring partnership, one that weathered the trials and tribulations of life with remarkable resilience. Kewalram often reflected on how Ganga's guidance had been a protective force, steering him away from pitfalls and keeping him grounded on the path of righteousness. Their fifty years of togetherness were not without their share of quarrels and disagreements, yet the joy of companionship far outweighed these fleeting moments of discord. Her passing marked a poignant turning point in his life—one that left a void impossible to fill.

"She would've loved seeing the kids like this," he would often remark to Leela, his voice heavy with sadness as he watched his grandchildren play in the garden.

"I know, Baba," Leela would reply softly, fully aware of how deeply he missed her mother.

The house was lively and full of activity, yet for Kewalram, it always felt a little quieter without Ganga's calming presence. She had been his rock, his unwavering support through every challenge life had thrown their way. Her absence was a silent grief he bore, a loss that left an ache he could never truly escape.

Many evenings, when the house grew quiet, Kewalram would settle into his favorite chair by the window, gazing out at the dusky sky. His thoughts would inevitably drift to Ganga—her soft laughter, the way she hummed while cooking, and the reassuring touch of her hand in his. He often found himself adrift in these memories, aching for the solace of her companionship.

"She would've told me to keep going," he sometimes murmured to himself, as if speaking to her unseen presence that lingered in the air around him.

Despite the love and lively chaos of family around him, the void left by Ganga's absence was ever-present, a quiet ache that never fully faded. She had been his unwavering companion for decades, standing steadfast through every joy and challenge. Without her, life felt different—quieter, lonelier—even with the family's efforts to fill the gap.

As the years passed, the house grew quieter. With Girdhari's family settled in the UK and visits from other relatives becoming less frequent, Kewalram's later years felt increasingly solitary. He still cherished Leela's presence and Mira's regular visits, but the lively energy of earlier times had faded. The once-bustling home transformed into a quiet retreat, a place where he often sat in reflection, thinking about the life he had built and the family he held dear.

"Baba, why don't you come stay with us for a few days?" Mira would occasionally suggest, her voice laced with concern.

Kewalram would respond with a gentle smile and a shake of his head. "This is my home," he'd say softly. "Your mother and I built this life together. It's where I belong."

And so, he stayed, finding solace in his memories, even as they often weighed heavily on his heart. Leela's caring though unintrusive presence partially alleviated his solitude His final year, after all the bustling moments of family life, was defined by quiet solitude. He cherished the visits from his daughters and the occasional drop-ins from extended family, but Ganga's absence was most acutely felt in the stillness of those later years. As time went on, the loneliness only deepened, settling into the fabric of his days.

In the twilight of his life, Kewalram Kanuga found peace. He had accomplished what he set out to do, both in his career and in his personal life. He had helped build something enduring—something that would be remembered long after the oilfields ran dry and the pipelines carried their final barrels of crude. His legacy lived on in the people of Duliajan, in the community he had nurtured, and in the lives of the oilmen and women who would always recall the pivotal role he played in shaping their world.

As he sat watching the sunset, he felt a quiet satisfaction, knowing he had left behind a legacy of more than just oil—a legacy of care, connection, and community. And for Kewalram, that was a legacy worth leaving.

Chapter 19:
The Final Farewell

On the 6th September , 2000, the nation mourned the loss of one of its most beloved figures, Shri Kewalram Boolchand Kanuga, fondly known as the "grand old man of the Indian oil industry."

At the age of 88, Kanuga left behind a legacy as remarkable as the life he had lived. Throughout most of his years, he was known for his unwavering energy and visionary spirit. Even at 83, his mind remained sharp, and his zest for life was undiminished. However, as time passed, the inevitable effects of aging began to take hold. The final five years of his life were marked by a gradual physical decline, a natural progression of advancing age.

Despite these challenges, Kanuga's fierce independence remained unwavering. When his children, motivated by love and concern, urged him to move in with them for better care and comfort, he firmly declined. For Kanuga, dignity was inseparable from self-reliance. He chose to remain in his own home, a place imbued with cherished memories and the essence of a life well-lived. To him, it was far more than just a house; it was a sanctuary he had lovingly built, a space where he could continue to preside as the master of his domain.

Even in his later years, Kanuga remained deeply connected to the people who mattered most in his life. His home was a haven of warmth and hospitality, where children, grandchildren, old friends, and colleagues were always welcomed. Whether gathering for a casual family meal or sharing laughter-filled moments of reminiscence, Kanuga greeted everyone with the same generosity and grace that defined him throughout his life. He embodied the essence of a true patriarch—not through authority, but through the love, care, and unity he inspired in those around him.

In the final years of his life, Kanuga stood as a living symbol of resilience. Though his physical strength waned, his spirit remained unyielding. His home continued to serve as a gathering place for family and friends, a testament to the enduring values he instilled in all who entered. He remained a steadfast presence, uniting those around him and leaving behind a legacy of love and connection that would endure far beyond his lifetime.

When news of his passing spread, it echoed through the halls of Oil India Limited—the very company he had shaped with his vision and leadership. His death marked not only the loss of a remarkable man but the end of an era. For many, Kanuga's name had come to symbolize dedication, innovation, and integrity. His influence extended well beyond the technicalities of the oil industry, leaving a lasting impact on the lives of everyone who worked with him and learned from his wisdom.

Among the many tributes that poured in, one stood out—a deeply moving and beautifully written obituary by U B Acharya, a retired Oil India executive who had later settled in Pune. Published in OIL News, Acharya's words perfectly captured the profound impact Kanuga had on those he worked with and the industry he helped shape. Acharya's tribute was not just a remembrance; it was a powerful testament to the profound respect and admiration Kanuga had earned throughout his career.

Kanuga's funeral was an emotional gathering, not just of people, but of hearts. Colleagues, friends, and family came together, each carrying a piece of the man who had given so much to the nation. Amidst the solemnity, it was his youngest daughter, Leela, whose simple yet poignant poem captured the shared sentiment of everyone present:

"With the first ever breath of life,

The friends... who had,

Promised to come someday,

Have since arrived.

To hold my hand... and lead me,

To regions unknown...

At the moment of this final parting,

I bid you life... goodbye."

Her words drifted softly through the crowd, carrying the weight of love, loss, and the inevitability of farewell. They not only reflected the man Kanuga had been but also the quiet grace with which he had embraced death. Leela's poem served as a reminder that, while Kanuga had been a father to his children, he had also been a father figure to countless others who had sought his guidance and support.

As the sun set, casting a soft golden light over the mourners, the reality of Kanuga's absence began to sink in. He was gone, but his presence lingered everywhere—in the streets of Duliajan, in the buildings he had helped create, and, most of all, in the lives he had touched. His passing marked not just the end of a life, but the closing of a chapter in the history of India's oil industry, a chapter that would be remembered for generations to come.

In the days that followed, life in Duliajan returned to its usual rhythm, but a reverent silence hung in the air—a shared recognition of the man who had shaped much of what the township had become. Conversations often turned to "Kanuga Sahab"—his name spoken with respect, his stories retold with warmth, and his legacy recalled with admiration.

Shri Kewalram Boolchand Kanuga's life was not defined by fleeting achievements, but by lasting impact. His leadership had elevated India's oil industry onto the global stage, but beyond that, he had touched lives, built communities, and inspired futures. Although he had said farewell to the world, the spirit of his work, his values, and his compassion would continue to resonate long after his passing.

Kanuga's passing was more than a farewell—it was a celebration of a life defined by unwavering dedication, passion, and love. While the nation lost a great man, his legacy remained etched in the hearts of those who knew him. It stood as a shining testament to what one individual could accomplish with vision, courage, and an unrelenting commitment to making a difference.

www.ingramcontent.com/pod-product-compliance
Lightning Source LLC
LaVergne TN
LVHW041948070526
838199LV00051BA/2943